Stella Duffy was born in London and brought up in New Zealand. Her three other novels featuring Saz Martin – *Wavewalker*, *Beneath The Blonde*, and *Fresh Flesh* – are also published by Serpent's Tail. She has written two other novels, *Singling Out The Couples* and *Eating Cake*, many short stories, several articles, two one-woman shows and, most recently, a stage play for Steam Industry, *crocodiles and bears*. She is also an actor, improvisor, comedian, and occasional radio presenter. She now lives in London.

ACCLAIM FOR *CALENDAR GIRL*

"There's a lot of lesbian lore and sex in it, but it is also a fast, witty and clever crime story, with cracking dialogue and exuberant characters" *The Times*

"Steamy erotic moments, some smart one-liners and a few digs at lesbian stereotypes . . . Stella Duffy is definitely a name to watch" *Forum*

"Lends a new dimension to trips to the supermarket" *Literary Review*

"A highly atmospheric, rhythmic narrative . . . a stylish book which also warns of the destructive power of lies and half-truths" *Gay Times*

"Unusual, cleverly constructed recital of deception in relationships . . . The downbeat denouement packs an unexpected, morbid wallop" *San Francisco Examiner*

"Each chapter is satisfying in itself, but leaves you on a cinema noir knife-edge. Don't start it at bedtime or you'll wind up with bags under your eyes" *Phase*

CALENDAR GIRL

Stella Duffy

Library of Congress Catalog Card Number: 99–63578

A full catalogue record for this book can be obtained from
the British Library on request

The right of Stella Duffy to be identified as
the author of this work has been asserted by her
in accordance with the Copyright, Designs and
Patents Act 1988

First published by Serpent's Tail 1994
4 Blackstock Mews, London N4 2BT
website: www.serpentstail.com

First published in this five-star edition, 1999

Printed in Great Britain by Mackays of Chatham, plc
Chatham, Kent

**For Shelley
– of course**

Thanks to Shelley Silas for her faith, love and for having green eyes, Yvonne Baker for her great enthusiasm and support, Jo Stones for having a life, Dolores Hoy, Len Baker, Emma Hill, Ruth Logan, Luke Sorba, Veronica Tattersall and Ilsa Yardley for assistance along the way, and to Pete Ayrton and Laurence O'Toole at Serpent's Tail for persistence in the face of alarming negativity.

CHAPTER 1

Lunch

She had long legs, big brown eyes, great tits and cheek-bones to cut bread on.

"A Kelly McGillis body" I was to say later to anyone who'd asked. And to lots who hadn't. She'd been brought by a friend to see me perform. A mutual friend. And there I was all post-show bounce and cleavage and over the top and there she was all legs and eyes and cheekbones. Impossible already. We flirted mildly, talked a lot, both made our jobs sound a little more glamorous than they were and then we parted. I turned down her offer of a ride home. Well, I'm obvious, but not that obvious. Besides, Vauxhall, via Richmond (to pick up her car from Esther's) on her way to Golders Green seemed a bit more demanding than was warranted by a first meeting. And this way I could rush home to tell the assortment of ex-lovers that I live with about the Woman with the Kelly McGillis body.

The woman I live with, with the Kelly McGillis body.

"No Esther" I said, "I do not want another lesbian virgin. I do not want to talk anyone else through coming out. I don't want to hug anyone else through career-trauma. I cannot take on the sexual responsibility, I do not wish to be, yet again, someone's First Lesbian Sex."

I paused for effect.

"Sexually liberated I may be, but the *Beginner's Guide to the Joys of Lesbian Sex* I'm not."

"Not any more anyway," sotto voce from Dolores which resulted in me pinching her thigh in what I hoped was a playful yet painful manner.

"But Maggie she isn't a lesbian virgin," slightly angry from Esther who certainly was and probably thought the idea of a lesbian virgin was kind of sweet, if not a state of being it was my solemn duty to eradicate.

"She's been with a woman – several – she's told her family, she's done girl-sex."

"Which is more than can be said for Esther." At which point I pinched Dolores again in what I hoped was a purely painful manner. Sometimes being good buddies with your ex-lover can be a pain in the thigh. Dolores' thigh. Esther looked at me with the imploring eyes of a straight, single, Jewish woman trying to match-make a Catholic and happily celibate dyke. It's an unusual position to be in and not an easy one to say no to.

The Woman with the Kelly McGillis body has long, taut thighs.

And so there she was. Brought along to see me at a gig by a mutual friend. And me being funny and witty and charming, which is of course nothing like my real neurotic, terrified self. Because doing stand-up comedy is ACTING – but tell that to someone who's just seen you perform for the first time, someone who has big dark eyes and olive skin, someone who looks older than their thirty-one years, someone who looks like a grown-up. Already it was impossible. We were doomed – I by her physiognomy, she by the first time I made her laugh – that she had achieved her cheek bones genetically and through no fault of her own and that I was getting paid to make her laugh mattered not at all. We were both available, and I managed to ignore all the usual warning signals, as I usually do:

"Don't do it just because she's the first good looking dyke you've seen in a year."

"Don't do it just because you fancy some sex and she looks like she might know how to do it."

"Don't do it just because you can" (Joelene).

The next day she called to ask me out.

Dolores gave me the message two Tuesdays later.

We arranged to meet for lunch.

I ironed a hole into Dolores' favourite shirt.

It's been weeks since I had lunch with the Woman with the Kelly McGillis body.

We had pasta.

I got up at 10am to get ready. I usually work until 1am, get to bed around three or four, so anything that can get me out of bed before the one o'clock news has to be special. I bathed and washed my hair to make my long, red curly curls curlier. I panicked and realised I was the ugliest woman in the world. I breathed into my crystal and took a large gulp of straight whisky. I realised I wasn't ugly, only plain and homely. I made three positive affirmations and about five negative ones. I smoothed myself into Dolores' brand new and as yet unsagging at the knees, jet-black leggings, and added a lycra vest (hint of underarm hair and more than a hint of Eternity). I figured I looked all right really, and I do have good eyes. I put on my cotton jacket, bouncy red basketball boots and got on my bike so that I would arrive flushed, breathless, a little late and just a little gorgeous.

She likes bodies to be virtually hairless.

As I said, we had pasta.

She hadn't said she'd pay so I added up my meal as we ordered, hoping she wouldn't choose expensive and that when it came time to split the bill my share wouldn't go over £15. I say £15 because that is all the money I had in the world, until Thursday's dole cheque. I exaggerate. Fifteen pounds and thirty six pence. Poetic licence. Halfway through lunch I had my second glass of wine, decided I wanted dessert and that owing her money wouldn't necessarily be a bad thing. It would at least give me a reason to see her again.

We talked for two and a half hours and I thought she must be important in her job to be allowed such a long lunch hour. We talked about families and growing up and travel and because we wanted to impress each other we didn't say much that was completely true, we embellished and gilded and stored up trouble for ourselves.

We talked and I realised I was blind, she had green eyes and wasn't especially tall and her tits weren't that big, though her legs are long and shapely. I altered my video image of her slightly and to "cheekbones to cut bread on" added "hip bones to pierce me on". For a modern lesbian feminist I can be disgustingly Catholic.

When the bill came it was over £40 so I discreetly went to powder my nose so she could discreetly pay the bill. I noticed she also discreetly asked for a receipt for expenses. She filofaxed me for easy reference. I wrote her number on an envelope I was carrying. The envelope contained the negatives of some photos of my ex-lover and me two summers ago in Brighton. I'd torn the photos up in winter, but held on to the inverted versions.

We arranged to meet in ten days time.

"Maggie, you're mad. Don't do it. I can't take it. The house can't take it. You can't afford the therapy. Maggie honey, ain't no nice Jewish girl from Golders Green gonna love you all the way through Yom Kippur."

Dolores sometimes thinks she's Tennessee Williams. But most of the time she thinks she's Gertrude Stein. I'm a great cook and hate recipe books. Dolores' mother was Catholic, her father is a rampant socialist, and she was named for the Spanish Civil War heroine Dolores Ibarruri before her father departed leaving her mother to bring up Dolly alone. When Dolores was twenty-eight she discovered her paternal grandmother. Her paternal grandmother was Jewish. That Dolores was therefore not strictly Jewish, that her grandmother's Judaism was limited to the names of the holidays (and not their dates), that her grandmother was a cantankerous, bigoted old bat, all mattered not a whit to Dolores who embarked on a study of her chosen religion with a fervour matched only by her devotion to the early writings of Rita Mae Brown. (Pre-Martina, Dolores hates sport, she doesn't like to sweat.) When Dolores discovered the infamous "Thank God I was not born a woman" prayer, her ardour cooled a little. Now she mostly confines her Judaism to celebrating the holidays and the Book of Ruth.

I kept Passover with the Woman with the Kelly McGillis body.

She called me that night and said she couldn't wait and could I come over on Friday night?

Dolores suggested taking a challah.
  I took pink champagne.

I always take pink champagne. It looks spontaneous and cute and is just expensive enough to suggest first-date abandon. It took me even longer to get ready this time because, as I was due to arrive at 10pm, it was rather unlikely that I'd go back home on the Northern Line before midnight, so I needed clothes I could wear the next day. I needed clothes I could be seduced out of. I sat outside her house for fifteen minutes before I rang the bell. I sat there and told myself that this didn't have to mean anything and that I was a grown up and could even just go home now if I really wanted to.

Time's winged chariot drove past and I realised I was late. I climbed the stairs, put on a brave and expectant face, rang the bell and handed her the champagne.

Champagne makes her throw up.

CHAPTER 2

Running for fun

Saz Martin woke up, rubbed her eyes and wished she didn't like gin quite so much. Or that she liked straight tonic a lot more. Sun was shafting its way through her cane blinds so she knew it had to be between 7 and 8am, the only time her fifth floor council flat received its dose of vitamin D. She rolled out of bed, retrieved her track suit bottoms and sports bra from the washing machine where they had been pointlessly thrown the morning before, stripped off the T-shirt she'd worn to bed, dressed and put the T-shirt on again. Socks and trainers added, she ran out the front door, pausing only to lock it with three different keys. Down five flights of stairs and out into the delights of early morning Camberwell. Rubbish and broken toys doing their best to hold back the greenery which threatened to cheer the place up. Only after she'd been running for a good couple of miles did she consult her watch – 7.45am.

"Not bad Martin, not bad at all. Four hours of dancing and revelry, two of which were unadulterated flirting, home all alone with not even a video to put you to sleep and now this after only three hours of dreamtime. Brown Owl would be proud!" She ran for half an hour, cold morning air hurting the back of her throat and stinging at the deepest pits of her lungs. She headed for the river and a semblance of rural idyll.

Saz turned at Vauxhall Bridge when the lead fumes became too heavy and made it home in time, via the new bagel bakery (two jam doughnuts), Safeway (fresh ground coffee) and newsagents (*The Guardian*, *Time Out*) in time to abuse the breakfast news the second time round.

After breakfast, sweet doughnut mingling with salt sweat on her lips, she showered, dumped all her clothes in the washing-machine, turned the washing-machine and answer-phone on and the telephone off. Then she went back to bed.

When Saz got up at midday, the sun had long gone, not only from her flat but from the whole of London and it had started to drizzle. Three years earlier Saz had discovered that the only really nice weather happened before other people went to work, so she started getting up to run in it. Running for fun. Unlike answering the phone. Answering the phone was not fun. Judging from the severity of the flashing light there were several messages waiting for her.

"Sarah, it's your mother. Darling, why don't you ever answer your phone? Daddy and I were hoping you'd come home for dinner some time this week. A little celebration for your birthday. Do you have a job at the moment? Because if not, we'd love to see you. I don't really know what to get you, Cassie just said maybe you could do with some money? But it seems so cold to me, anyway dear perhaps you could give me a call, um and . . . Cassie said she didn't think you were seeing anyone, but if you are then maybe you'd like to bring them . . . I mean her . . . home too? That is, if you are . . . well I'd best be off now, take care and hope you're not suffering with hayfever like Dad. God Bless darling."

"Ms Martin, it's Colleen from the Enterprise Allowance office. Perhaps you could come in some time next week –

it's almost the end of the first six months of your business and I'd like to go through your quarterly accounts with you. Please call to arrange an appointment as soon as possible."

"Saz, it's Cassie. Mother's been harassing me about your birthday, I don't know what you want, I said they should give you cash, hope that's OK. Look do you fancy baby-sitting this Wednesday only Tony wants to go out, get completely pissed and then ravish me and you wouldn't want to stop us from enjoying anything as married and juicily heterosexual as that would you? Let me know, only quickly cos otherwise I'll have to pay someone which would be distressing and probably mean you'd only get a cheap and shoddy birthday present, instead of merely a shoddy one! Bye."

"Saz, Claire here, was I pissed last night or did I make a complete fool of myself sober? I'll stick to the former if it's all right with you. Let's do something civilised tomorrow like walking in the park and having tea, don't worry, I'll pay, and then I can tell you all about the damn fine sex I had last night. Hah!"

"Cassie again, Mum also wants to know if you're doing it with anyone. So does Tony. I don't. I think eleven months of celibacy is wonderful and healthy and all I want to know is, will you babysit? Call me quickly, my loins can't stand the suspense."

"Hello, Miss Martin, ah . . . you don't know me but I was given your number by a friend, well an acquaintance really, and you see the thing is, oh God I hate these machines, don't you? . . . actually I'm ringing to see if you could help me, I mean I'd like to employ you, that is if you still do the sort of work my friend said you do . . . I mean I've never employed anyone to . . . spy on anyone before, well it's not spying is it, more like checking up . . . well, perhaps you could call me – John Clark, ah . . . and maybe you could be discreet . . . it's a work number . . ."

He waffled on a bit more, left the number and apologised again, Saz wrote his number on the back of her hand as the answerphone bleeped four times signalling the end of the messages. She poured fresh coffee.

"Thank God for continuous tape."

She then dialled her sister's number.
    "Cassie, it's me . . . no, I just woke up . . . no, I was not having sex, I gave that up remember? I went dancing and drinking and slept for three hours, ran for one and then slept for another three. I now feel fresh and alive and willing to commit myself to several hours of torture at the sticky fingers of your three brats . . . yes, I thought you'd be happy for me. Look, will you tell Mum, I do definitely prefer cash to anything else she might think I need, it'll make my Enterprise Allowance 'supervisor' very happy – I'll tell her it came from some old lady who needed me to find her long lost son . . . well, whatever – I need cash and I have enough tupperware and 'nice linen' to last me several millennia in suburbia, let alone the single lesbian life in the inner city . . . yes, I said single and I did mean single, anyway I think I might have a job . . . I don't know yet, I have to call him back . . . yes, it's a man . . . well, of course I won't do it if it's an ex-husband. Look babe, I've got to go and call this bloke back, when you speak to Mother don't tell her I'm working, I think she's prefers me unemployed and poor to unsafe and working . . . No, I'm not unsafe, it's just that's how she sees it. OK give my love

to Tony, tell him not to worry, I prefer my brothers-in-law bald. Bye."

Saz hung up and dialled Claire's number.

"Smart, Holland and Swift, Solicitors, can I help you?"

The idea of Claire Holland, old school friend, dizzy blonde, raving pisshead and the first of Saz's friends to come out, as a really truly grown up solicitor (with receptionist and secretary) never failed to stun Saz.

"Can I speak to Ms Holland, please?"
    "I'm sorry, Ms Holland's in a meeting at the moment, can I take a message?"
    "No, it's fine, just say Saz called, I'll call her back. Just ask her if her headache's OK."
    "Oh, her headache's gone now, she threw up not long after her first meeting, ordered a BLT and tomato juice and is feeling just fine. I'll tell her you called. Bye Ms Martin."

Saz called the number on her hand. The voice on the other end of the phone told her she was being held in a queue and would she mind holding. Saz didn't mind holding, what she did mind was having to listen to 'Greensleeves' as she did so.

"Can I speak to John Clark please?"
    "John's not here."
    "Well, could you take a message please?"
    "No."
    "I'm sorry?"
    "I said 'No', I can't take a message because John's not here, he doesn't work here any more, he quit."

"When?"

"About half an hour ago, took 'voluntary redundancy'. They've been offering it for over a year and he decided to take it two weeks ago, only he forgot to tell me until this morning. I told him he might as well go now as far as I'm concerned. So he did. Now look dear, I've got plenty to do with the assistant manager having just quit on me without spending all my lunch hour answering stupid questions, so if you're his girlfriend, then I'm bloody sorry for you, but why don't you just try calling him at home? I'm sure Mrs Clark would love to hear from you."

"Ah, his wife?"

"Yes darling, wife. You're not the first to have called this morning, seems all the chickens are coming home to roost, no wonder he's been looking so bloody worried. Now come on sweetheart, bugger off, I've got work to do."

"Just one last thing, where am I calling?"

"Where? That's a silly bloody question isn't it, luv? This is British Telecom. Anything else I can help you with or can I get on with something that actually matters?"

"No, that's plenty thanks, unless you have Mr Clark's home number?"

"Darling, I've got all the numbers here. You probably do too. This is BT remember? Every Mr Clark in London. There's about three thousand of them in the phone book. I suggest you start looking."

He laughed and hung up.

Saz poured more coffee and turned on the TV. Helen Daniels was looking puzzled too.

CHAPTER 3

Supper

I handed her the champagne, warm from my nervous hands and she motioned me inside. No kiss. No hug. Had I misread her totally? Was this just a 10.15pm visit for coffee? And if so how soon could I reasonably leave to get the last tube home?

The sitting room assaulted me with a garish mix of colours and sensations – Persian carpet, geranium oil burning, Liza Minnelli singing, plants and books. Books everywhere. Two deep on bookshelves, on and under the tables, covering the mantelpiece, piled on the floor in completely random arrangement. She obviously hadn't heard of the Dewey Decimal System. The place looked less ordered than Dolores' diary, which was saying something.

I waited for her to speak.

I'm sitting opposite the Woman with the Kelly McGillis body now. But I don't wait for her to speak anymore.

"My nephew doesn't understand why my mummy doesn't make me tidy my room."

She moved some cushions from under a pile of papers (*The Guardian*, *The Independent* and *New Moon*) and told me to sit down. She put the champagne in the fridge and handed me white wine. Chilled. She offered nuts and crisps. Japanese rice crackers. We mentioned work. She told me her boss was leaving, that she was nervous, scared she'd lose her job. I imagined her flat cost a lot in mortgage repayments. It was big and would have been spacious if not for all the books. Three doors led off the room we were in – one to a large kitchen, red and black, tiled floor and walls. Huge state-of-the-art fridge (ice maker) and cooker (eye-level grill). Four shelves of cookery books. Titles in Japanese and Italian. Gleaming sets of crockery. Shiny glasses. Six of everything. Whole sets, nothing broken. Microwave and blender and juice extractor shone, spotlit from lights hidden in recesses in the ceiling. I tried not to look too impressed, too poor. As if I too could afford a kitchen from the pages of one of those magazines. As if I could afford one of those magazines.

"I love big kitchens," I told her. "I expect you love cooking in here, all these gadgets, all this space."

She inherited the flat lock, stock, barrel and fully furnished from her aunt. No payment involved. And she never cooks. The only thing she added to the place were the books.

Books which now line the shelves of our home. Neatly. In alphabetical order.

We exchanged pleasantries for a painfully long ten minutes. Work, weather and the United Nations. Just as I began to plan my route home and how I would manage to fend off Dolores' questions, she grabbed my hair, pulled me to her.

She said "Kiss me."

So I did.

We began gently. Soft kisses on her full lips. Soft kisses on my soft lips. She pulled at me, sucking my lower lip, sucking as if it was my nipple. Sucking my lips like I used them to give nourishment, not to take it. Her tongue tasted the cool white wine on my teeth.

She opened the door to the bedroom, as I took in the cupboards – at least ten of them, the mirrors – one on each wall and the bedspread – Indian, red and purple, woven with threads of gold and silver, she removed her clothes.

I found her again between the black sheets. I started to undress.

She said "No, slowly. Do it for me. Do it slowly."

Typical. Bloody audiences. They think actors want to perform all the time.

They're right.

I undid my boots, slowly pulling the laces from their holes, trying not to seem any more Jungian than necessary. I slipped off my jacket – hung it on the back of the door. Between two dressing-gowns, both silk, one red, one emerald green. I wondered which I'd use in the morning. I was wearing an ankle length black dress. Fitted bodice, then full from a drop waist. I undid the buttons and let the dress fall to the ground. I didn't pick it up. There was a mirror just above her head where she lay in bed. I watched her watching me. And watched myself being watched. Saw my body. Sheer black tights under a black lace camisole. Pink nipples just blushing through the black. My reflection, like Alice in the looking glass, half believing the cliché I presented. I saw the body she longed to touch. I touched the body she longed to touch. I saw my hand tempting her against the black lace. I saw the full white cleavage. My body. With one movement I removed both camisole and tights and stood before her naked. Pubes vibrant testimony to the authenticity of my red hair.

She nodded and smiled, "Very good."

I laughed, "Very practised."

I sat beside her on the bed, began to trace the line of her collarbone. The line down to her breasts.

We were taking this slowly. Each editing the passages we'd written for this night. Editing two separate accounts of the same situation to make one homogenous version. Homogenous sounds like milk. Pasteurised. Cleaned. Our scripts were neither milky white nor germ free. But for one moment they were the same.

And for this moment they are the same too. Because she isn't arguing with me now.

I pulled the sheets back and gently lowered myself on to her body. I lay on top of her. We breathed in rhythm. She in, me out. Me in, she out. My still soft nipples found hers erect and hard. Her hip bones, narrower than mine, fitted between mine, my flesh meeting her bone. Hip bones to pierce me on, St Sebastian, hip bones to pierce me. My toes reached down to her ankles, her longer legs passing mine. With my hands I stroked the side of her body, she began to touch my back. Touching my back, scratching my back. Kneading my pliant, compliant flesh. Needing my flesh. Her hands found my hair and pulled it, sharp so my neck and body arched back, pushing my pubic bone into hers. She pulled harder, pushing me harder into her own body. With her hands in my hair, I became the lever with which she made herself come, as I rocked faster and faster on top of her I saw myself in the mirror above her bed. Saw the crown of her head, saw her hands in my hair, locked into my locks, saw my white throat, so vulnerable, so exposed, saw my breasts, thrusting forward as they crashed down on to hers. Saw myself the wave crashing on her shore. She came with a violent shudder and threw me off her. I rested as the aftershocks ran through her and she came round. Came to. Came back to herself. Came after coming. A while later she opened her eyes and smiled at me. A languorous smile, a sated smile, the smile of a plan well executed.

It's a smile I know well. It's the smile I smile to myself these days. Sometimes.

I asked her if she came.

"Darling, you're the performer, not me. Of course I came, and came and came, what did you think that was? Going?"

I didn't know what answer to give so I kissed her instead. I kissed her mouth and her breasts and her navel. I was about to kiss further but she pulled me up to her and said,

"Not tonight sweetheart. I promise in future I'll give you plenty of chances to play with me, but tonight is the first night so tonight we take turns. We do it evenly. Share and share alike."

She ran her hand over my breast and swiftly down to my stomach, then without pausing she held me round the neck, with one hand she pulled my hair fierce and tight, with the other she fucked me. Fast. Hard. And deep. So deep I couldn't quite catch my breath. Between gasps I tried to speak.

"Don't you . . . believe . . . aaah . . . believe in . . . ooh . . . oh God . . . don't you believe in pre . . . in preliminaries? . . . oh fuck!"

"Shut up."

She kissed me, her tongue far into my mouth. I lay on my back. Legs splayed, one arm pinned behind me, the other behind her, my body slightly arched where she still pulled my hair taut, her tongue thrusting against mine, her whole hand plumbing my depths. I felt myself start to come. She felt it too and leaving her fingers in me, found my clitoris with her thumb. Her fingers inside me and her thumb outside of me pinched me between them in frantic, circling jabs, I saw the long dark tunnel, felt myself being rushed to the white wall at the end of it. Felt myself about to smash headlong into it, and just as I hit the wall, melted inwards, down from my toes and fingers into the centre of my sex, felt the blood rush to the centre, the way the sea drags back from the beach, miles and miles back, so it can build itself huge, minutes before the tsunami crashes on the shore.

The wave crashed. I drowned. She licked her fingers and smiled.

"Mmm, salty but not quite kosher. Good shabbas anyway."

She fell asleep and I lay, marvelling at the ability some people have of giving their all and then just giving up to sleep. It takes me hours to wind down after sex. That's why I like to have sex in the morning, it sets me up for the day.

I'm watching her now. It's dawn and she lies there quiet as I touch myself.

I watch her silent body as I slowly take myself down that tunnel.

CHAPTER 4

Brain Workout

Two weeks after her birthday Saz Martin sat across a table from John Clark. Apparently he'd called again three times but her mother had managed to be cold enough to give Saz money for her birthday and Saz had managed to be cold enough to use it to get her answerphone fixed. Overuse had rendered it useless, so she'd missed quite a few calls for a couple of weeks.

John Clark had rung sounding harried and tired and Saz had agreed to meet him at a café near Leicester Square. She leant back on the hard bench seat they were sharing with the other late afternoon customers. Refugees from office hour mentality.

Middle-aged, grey-faced and obviously ill at ease. John Clark picked up his glass of iced water and put it down again for the third time without drinking.

"So you see, it's unheard of for me not to see her for this long – four weeks. She's never not contacted me before. And I feel so strange about it. And well, now I don't know what to do and I think . . . I mean I know she's in trouble. She needs help but I don't know how to help her. So when this bloke at work mentioned he knew someone who . . . well, women like you. I mean people doing what you do. I thought, maybe you could help me. . .?"

Saz finished her espresso and motioned to the counter for another. She stared out the window at the drizzle, then shook her head as she looked down at the notepad on the table in front of her.

"Now let me see if I've got this straight. You, Mr Clark, are telling me that you have a very best friend, a woman you would give your life for, a woman who is the only person who understands you. And vice versa. Right so far?"

John Clark nodded and played with the ice floating in his glass, Saz continued.

"This woman asked you to accept voluntary redundancy from your job so that you would get quite a few thousand pounds worth of golden handshake. Sixteen thousand pounds in fact, most of which you then 'loaned' to her to get her out of a financial jam she wouldn't even tell you about. A financial jam you didn't even know about until the night she came up with the idea. And you left the money for her – cash – in a left luggage locker at Charing Cross Station. And that was six weeks ago now. Yes?"

"Not quite, they'd been hassling us to make up our minds about the redundancy offer for ages. I'd talked it over with my wife and she thought it might be the best thing – pay off most of the mortgage and we'd still have some left over to keep us for a bit. And something to give the kids – university, all that to consider . . ."

"Yes. But to get back to your friend?"

"I told you. She said she was in trouble and it would be best for both of us if I knew nothing about it."

"Hold on, you're skipping the most important bit. This 'best friend' is someone whose home you have never been to, whose occupation you have no idea of, whose name you don't even know, who you've only ever met for dinner on the first and third Friday of every month for the past three years. You have never had a phone number for her, she was never more than three minutes late and she's only ever cancelled three dinners in all that time."

"Yes. I don't see why you think it's so strange . . ."

"No, no – please wait. And best of all you've never slept with her. I mean really Mr Clark, forgive me if it all sounds just a little bit far-fetched!"

"I know. You're right. And that's why I couldn't go to the police. But I tell you Miss Martin. . ."

"Ms," Saz corrected him automatically.

"Sorry, Ms Martin. It's the truth and I know something is wrong. I can feel it. I know her very well. She wouldn't lie to me. There were certain things – her work, our lovers, my marriage, childhood – which we never spoke of. At least not the specifics of those subjects. She said that way, we'd never be tempted to lie to each other. We talked about art and music, writing and philosophy. We have had a relationship for three years. We understood each other. We talked about feelings. And I can feel that something is wrong."

Saz looked at John Clark. An ordinary man in middle age in his grey office suit – the sort of man she'd seen and immediately forgotten so many times before. The sort of man who might have a fling with the temp or flirt with the babysitter. The sort of man with a hefty mortgage and a couple of teenage kids. With a willing but secretly frustrated wife. The sort of man who had two weeks holiday a year, and that holiday was planned and paid for in February. This was not the sort of man with the imagination to make up a story like this. Not at £25 an hour of Saz's time. And this was not the sort of man to lie about something big. Probably not anyway.

"OK Mr Clark. I believe you. At least I figure I might as well believe you. But if I'm to even begin trying to find your friend I need to know a lot more than this. Don't you have any idea what her name is? I mean, what did you call her? 'Hey you'?"

"No, after our third dinner she came up with an idea, I was to call her whatever the month was called. You know like April, May, June . . ."

"Bit much in December wasn't it?"

"Well, it only happened twice a year."

"I suppose so. OK, no name. Where did you meet?"

"In a bookshop. We were both browsing. I asked her to have a coffee with me. She had lots of bags with her. I assumed she was just back from holiday."

"Did you ask where she'd been?"

"No."

"But she agreed to have a coffee with you?"

"Yes, we got on, I suggested we have dinner. It's that simple."

"Yeah, right. What about the restaurants, whose name were they booked under?"

"Mine, I paid too so I couldn't tell you what credit cards she had – has – or even if she has them, she always carries cash."

Saz started on her second espresso and turned her notepad over purposefully.

"Right then, Mr Clark. Here's something you will be able to answer. Give me a complete physical description. I want to know everything. From her height to her weight to any little – it doesn't matter how little – scars or marks she may have had. Fire away. I want the works."

John Clark frowned, closed his eyes and began.

"She's medium height, 5'6" or 5'7", not taller. Medium build, 126 to 130lbs. She doesn't wear high heels. Doesn't need to, she's got great legs. The rest of her body is good, I think she goes to a gym, she works out somewhere anyway. But her legs are the best. She has very long, shapely legs. Nice lips, she wears hardly any makeup, just a touch of lipstick, no mascara. Orange is her favourite colour. She has long pale blonde hair. Short fringe. Well, shortish. It depends. When she's happy she goes to get it cut, but if she's having a difficult time, not feeling particularly at ease with herself, she lets it grow. She says it gives her something to hide behind. To cover her eyes. Her amazing eyes. It's hard to tell what colour they are at times, they're so dark, as if the whole eye is taken up by her pupil, but in the light you can see them clearly, they're brown. Very dark brown. They're beautiful. She's beautiful Ms Martin, and she's my friend. Please . . . help me?"

John Clark looked up at Saz.

Saz reached across the table and took his hand.

"Look Mr Clark, I know you're upset and you're scared and you can't bear to think the worst but whenever you let your mind go that's all you can think. I know you're having an appalling time right now. But you've got to hold it together. You left your job two weeks ago. You've got sixteen thousand pounds redundancy payment, a mortgage, two kids and a wife to support who probably doesn't yet even know you left work voluntarily, let alone that you gave over two thirds of your redundancy payment away as a 'loan' to a woman who's now disappeared. Am I right?"

John Clark nodded.

"Right, and added to that you've got me to pay, so now let's get on with it. I need you to remember stuff. The time she didn't meet you, why was that?"

"She hurt herself. She broke her ankle."

"Great. We can check hospitals and emergency records. When was it?"

"Three years ago, only our fifteenth dinner."

"Wonderful. I can spend the next nine months checking hospital records. Anything else while I'm at it, anything she was allergic to? Any medication she took?"

"I'm not sure. She did see a homeopath for a while. About two years ago. It made it very difficult to eat out. She couldn't have alcohol or spicy foods or even coffee. It was for headaches I think. And she got hayfever – sometimes."

"Sometimes?"

"Well, we went to a couple of outdoor concerts one year – I arranged them as a special treat – you know the ones, Kenwood, Alexandra Palace, she especially liked the jazz – so do I. Jazz is something of a hobby of mine Ms Martin, you see I . . ."

"The hayfever, Mr Clark?"

"Oh yes, well she got hayfever. Once. Sneezed almost constantly for a couple of hours. I had to take her away – I offered to take her home but she wouldn't let me. Made me drop her off at the tube."

"Can you remember which one?"

"Not offhand, somewhere in North London obviously – probably the Northern Line, we were at Kenwood when she started sneezing if I remember correctly."

"And this was?"

"Summer before last."

"This is good Mr Clark, specifics are good. Now what I want you to do is this. Go home. Try and be nice to your wife. Don't tell her about June or July or whatever her name is, she'll never understand and she'll definitely think you were having an affair. In fact she'll probably think we're having an affair. Check your diaries, I want times, dates and places of every meeting the two of you ever had.

Can you do that? Do you keep your diaries?"

"Well, yes of course."

Saz looked at John Clark's grey suit and smiled.

"Somehow I thought you might. Let me know as soon as you've compiled a comprehensive list of places and dates. And write more about what she looks like. You might think of more if you try to be a little poetic. Try thinking romantically."

"But it wasn't like that!"

"Well, philosophically then. Think about her – clearly. See what vision she conjures up for you. I want to know what she wanted you to feel about her. We need to know what she thought to get any insight on who she was. Is, sorry. Try and remember if she's mentioned any shops to you – the place she gets her hair cut maybe, or any bags she might have carried her shopping in. I want to know everything. Any waiters or waitresses she might have been especially friendly with. And any foods she didn't eat – might help if she's funny about certain foods – religious or something like that. She's your friend so lots of things will seem insignificant to you, but not to me, right? I need to know everything you know about her. And more. Her name for a start. Get back to me in a couple of days time. OK?"

John Clark nodded and Saz hurried out of the cafe into the grey London drizzle, the spring in her step belying the weight on her mind. Once she was out of his range of sight she slowed down and followed the pedestrian flow into the tube, thinking it over.

"And John Clark, I'll take the interesting jobs. I'll check the gyms . . . and the morgues –

"Got any bodies with stunning brown eyes?"

"No, but the ones who got punched to death have got black ones!"

"That's the way Saz, faced with the completely impossible, joke about it! No Mama, I'm just fine. My job's not unsafe at all. Weird, but not unsafe. Not yet anyway . . . Damn you September, the left luggage at Charing Cross Station and not even giving him your real name! How naff film-noir can you get?"

CHAPTER 5

Milch und Fleisch

For three months we saw each other at least three times a week. Three nights a week. Nights that extended into afternoons and the next night. For three months we saw each other three times a week, seven nights a week. Dolores wanted to find a way to hate her but she couldn't. The Woman with the Kelly McGillis Body was quiet and accommodating and tidy and polite. At my house. In her own domain she was loud and orgasmic and a slattern. I was loud and orgasmic everywhere, upstairs, downstairs and in my lady's chamber (especially in my lady's chamber), but nowhere, never, was I a slattern.

Towards the end of the third month I had a lot of work, for about three weeks we only saw each other in bed. I'd come home to my bed or hers at about 2am, we'd fuck, sleep and she'd get up for work at eight. We were tired and irritable and hungry for more of each other. We ate each other up.

It was November. I'd just finished a run of particularly demanding late night gigs (nasty students, lots of boys, lots of alcohol) and she arrived to pick me up. I got in the back of the battered old red sports car and saw a full plastic bag in the back.

"What's that? Can't find a rubbish bin in North London?"

"No" she replied "It's your clothes. We're going away for a few days."

Charmed by the fact that someone had actually been as romantic as I'd always hoped someone – anyone – would, I fell asleep and slept beside her as she drove through the night. We arrived at about 7am. A "Women's Guest House" in Yorkshire. Two up, two down and the whole of the down was ours. The landlady, looking rather more like someone's mum than a northern dyke, showed us through the 'separate entrance' to the ground floor of her house. Sitting room backed on to kitchen/diner. Bathroom backed on to bedroom. The sitting-room and bathroom were both grey, damp and freezing. But then, we had no intention of sitting and little desire to wash the perfume of each other from our bodies. However, it was cold and Yorkshire is no place to be in November without central heating. Or a partner. The fridge in the corner of our own private kitchen was crammed with cold meats and vegetarian selections – pasta, cheeses, pâté. Fresh milk and orange juice. Honey smoked turkey. Meat and milk jostling for space on the same shelf. But I didn't know that mattered, then. A fruit bowl filled with winter miracles of mango and pineapple. Fresh bread. We stayed five nights and every morning there was fresh bread and milk. We decided our landlady was either a witch or Jesus. But I said she couldn't be Jesus because while there were plenty of loaves, there wasn't a fish in sight. The Woman with the Kelly McGillis Body didn't know what I was talking about.

French windows, too cold to have migrated this far north, looked out on a morning moor. Bleak and blue in the faint half light. The landlady left us and we made love on the kitchen floor, 1960s cold lino, 1990s hot sex. She, exhausted from the drive and more, fell asleep naked in my arms. I half dragged her body to the bed and we slept through the morning. We stayed in bed for the rest of the day. The curtains stayed apart to let the moor in. We stayed together to keep our lust in. The wind played on my emotions and I called her Cathy for the rest of the week. She, halfway through Jane Eyre, called me Helen. I, having read the book three times before I was fourteen, hadn't the heart to tell her it was a bad choice. We slept soundly in our red room and the next day made the pilgrimage to the parsonage. I cried because she wouldn't come with me to Top Withins, nor would she let me walk alone. She said it was too cold and too far and might get dangerous. I said what if they'd said that to Emily? That you could never be sure that anything might not turn out to be dangerous eventually. She said I was being swept along with the passion of it all and not being sensible. That I was being melodramatic.

I wasn't. You never can be sure.

She cried at Charlotte's tiny slippers. Cried both because her own feet were too big and because Charlotte was long dead and her feet were long cold.

The Woman with the Kelly McGillis Body has very cold feet today.

We walked through the parsonage hushed and excited, trying to catch inspiration. But genius is not a contagious disease and neither she nor I died of consumption on the moors.

We drank in The Black Bull imagining the stocky and talent-free Branwell wasting himself at the bar. Wasting his sisters at the bar. I wanted to waste myself at the bar but she said there were places to see. She drove me to York Minster where I lit a candle and she muttered Hebrew to protect herself from the cult of the Messiah. We ate in teashops, stopped to buy pottery and drove back across Ilkley Moor at midnight as a full moon rose above us.

All this really happened. It was such magic and yet now, as I ask her to remember those first few days, she will not even answer me. She cannot even answer me.

I sent Dolores a postcard of the slippers and Esther one of other people's gravestones.

We ate at a just-opened first class hotel on a deserted moor with a heated swimming pool and no guests. We had drinks with three of the staff and were the only patrons until 10.30pm. She ate pheasant and tore the flesh from the dead bird's bones. That night she tore the flesh from mine and sucked on the marrow of my heart. I was in lust and love and impatient.

I am impatient.

From the Brontë Parsonage to Sylvia Plath's grave. I like my writers dead before forty. Over a hundred years of literature in a five-minute car ride. I asked at the Haworth Tourist Information Centre about Sylvia. They sold lovely plastic models of the Brontë sisters and delightful group portraits of the three of them clustered around Branwell but they'd never heard of Sylvia Plath. The girl at the desk had to go and ask her boss. Apparently he could read. She came back to me.

"Was she married to a poet?"

I turned white "Mmm."

"Well yes, we do have a note here. Under Hughes. He's a poet, don't know about her. A Mrs Hughes buried in the Old Church – is that the one you mean?"

I turned red. "Her name was Sylvia Plath. She was a great poet. A very great poet in her own right. You illiterate cow."

The Woman with the Kelly McGillis Body led me, blind with rage, from the office.

I was livid. Red, white and blue for the America Sylvia had left and the distant sky was black for the shoes of the man listed instead of her.

We took the long road across the moor and some very tight hairpin bends.

We trawled through about four cemeteries – Catholic, Methodist, Baptist – Jewish hackles rising at my side. Then we found the ruined churchyard. Two churches stood side by side. One dark and locked. The other an open ruin. In it about six cats played, two older and the others only just grown from kittens. Each one with nine times to die. One attached itself to us, it purred around her legs until the Woman with the Kelly McGillis Body pushed it away.

She hates cats. She said she was allergic to them. She made me leave my cat behind when we moved in together. She's allergic to feathers and pollen and dust too. But I'm leaning against a feather pillow now and she's not sneezing at all.

It was 6pm and dusk and I was nervous. Thick banks of cloud and the ruined church doing their best Hammer horror impression. My Christianity-sensitive Jewess was positively scared. I wanted to go back for her. She wanted to go on for me. We followed the cat.

This really happened.

The cat took us to a cemetery on the other side of the standing church. Graves were arranged in orderly rows. The sun was nearly set and we followed the cat to Sylvia. Again my sensibilities were stormed, in the dusk-light the tombstone wording read "Sylvia Plath-Hughes".

I thought I was the first person to have been offended by it.

We both cried this time. I left a wildflower and the Woman with the Kelly McGillis Body left two stones. One for herself and one for Sylvia's Jewish-identified pain.

We drove back to London the next day. It was Friday and she had to be back to make it to her parents' for dinner. She went every week without fail. I've never met them. They hate the idea of me. A woman and not Jewish. I'm not sure which sin they hate more.

She hasn't been to them for two weeks in a row now, I wonder when they'll get up the courage to ring me and ask how she is?

We drove without stopping. She fucked me twice with her left hand as she drove. Car in fifth gear, me in tenth. Safe sex, unsafe driving. I came three times on the motorway. She dropped me off at my house and my flat-mates were, unusually, out. I couldn't bear the thought of being alone, of not sleeping with her and made sweetly violent, soft, harsh love to her on the couch in front of the gas fire.

She kissed me and drove north again. I cried from exhaustion and loneliness. She called me from a phone box on her

way home and said "I want to live with you. I don't want
to live apart from you."

I promised she'd never have to.

I went to bed ecstatic. Finally a lover who took me as seriously as I took her. Finally a lover who loved me back.

We vowed never to sleep apart again.

And we never have. Even now I cuddle up beside her. But
although she's wearing a warm jumper and it's not
Yorkshire, she's very, very cold.

CHAPTER 6

Footwork

Saz spilled out of the rush hour tube and went straight to the gym. Concentrating hard to ignore the beautiful glistening bodies, she started to work. Nothing like adrenalin flowing through the body to get the brain working clearly. Half an hour later and sweating herself, she walked straight past her usual Tuesday night flirtation and downstairs to the pool. After thirty lengths she was exhausted and had a nearly formulated plan of action. She showered, dressed and hurried out into the evening. The slow walk home through Brixton gave her time to both dry her hair and order her thoughts.

In her flat she made for the phone and called Gary. Her sister's ex-boyfriend of twelve years ago. Then a radical and angst-ridden biology student, now a part-time actor and full time office worker at St Catherine's House, Registrar of Deaths Division. Cassie and Gary were no longer in touch, but Saz bought him tickets to the National occasionally and a lot of coffee afterwards so he could tell her what a lot of pretentious crap went on in the theatre. Except when it was performed by his company, in which case it was ground-breaking but severely under-funded. And about once a year Gary was able to help Saz.

"Yes, Gary, it is a long shot, but see what you can do. If you can't be bothered going through the names yourself, just give me the list and I'll peruse them at my leisure. Thanks babe, I owe you one."

Having requested a list of the names of all the women in the twenty-five to thirty-five age bracket who had died in London in the past six weeks, Saz put down the phone. She well knew that despite Gary's protests she would have the list by the day after tomorrow, she also knew this favour would cost a little more than the National. A night in Stratford more like.

She then called Helen and Judith, old friends, coupled for five years – a minor record in Saz's eyes and that of the two policewomen. They agreed to meet her when Judith came off duty.

Saz went to bed for an hour to give her brain a chance to catch up.

Ten thirty saw her wide awake, washed and looking forward to a night out. Her black lycra body threading its way through a similarly dressed crowd to the corner table where Helen and Judith sat. Helen dark, Judith fair, both bowing to the muggy, damp summer evening by wearing as little as possible under their matching cropped black leather jackets and above their heavy DMs.

"I'll get them," Saz called when she was within shouting distance.
    "Too late," answered Helen, pointing to the three double gin and tonics sitting on the table before her.

Saz kissed the women, picked up her glass and tapped it against theirs, the three of them shouting, "To Plato!"

Saz had met Helen and Judith three years earlier on a
women's poetry course. Held deep in the wilds of West
Yorkshire, all three had eagerly signed up for what was
billed as a 'Wild Weekend for Women – Greek poetry as
you've never known it before! Discover your soul before it
discovers you! Women Only!' Unfortunately it wasn't
quite the weekend of Sapphic abandonment they'd been
hoping for. The poetry was definitely Greek but none of
the three women had ever anticipated wanting to read
Plato – in the original – with thirteen Philosophy dons
before. Sensing a kindred spirit (and one without a car)
Judith and Helen had offered Saz a ride back to London
on the Saturday morning and all three had done a bunk
just as the other women settled down to three hours on
'Plato – The Soul – Where Is It Located?' During the ride
back, Saz transformed her idea of 'pigs' (or at least of
sows) and discovered more about the hidden life of the
lesbian community than she'd learnt in ten years on 'the
scene'.

"So, girls, how's life in the sty?"

"Not bad, sweetheart, not bad. How's life in
Camberwell? Still celibate?"

"As ever, Hells, you can't manage to say 'hello' without
enquiring after my sex life, God knows why you work in
the police when an 'investigative journalist' post at *The
Sun* would suit you far better."

"Can't help myself, Saz. If I know whether you're doing
it or not at this moment, then I won't have to worry about
putting my foot in it unnecessarily later."

"Can you put a foot in necessarily?" Judith asked her
lover.

"No darling, not unless it's the boot. But if you don't trot
off to the bar and get us all another gin, you won't be
allowed to wear mine ever again."

Judith made her way to the bar and Saz filled Helen in on the details of her non-existent sex life. By the time Helen had given Saz the details of her and Judith's extremely existent sex life, Judith had clawed her way to the front of the bar and had made it back with the drinks. Sex talk over, Saz told them everything about the John Clark story adding that, though it sounded ludicrous, she did believe him and that she'd enrolled Gary's help, though with a lot less background information.

Judith rolled her eyes when Saz had finished and let out a gasp of disbelief.

"No, he's just got to be an ex-husband or a pimp or some kind of sleaze-bag. This story is just too silly. I mean it's the 1990s, what sort of woman calls herself September for God's sake?"

"Come on babe," countered Helen, "What sort of woman calls her lover her flatmate? What sort of woman lied only last night to her mother about the nature of her sexuality?"

"Oh please don't start again, that's not fair. Anyway, surely you're not suggesting that January's mother is such a harridan that though she's really a lesbian she has dinner twice a month with a man she won't tell her name to, and she wants to get sixteen thousand quid out of?"

"No, but if sixteen thousand quid would get you brave enough to finally come out to your family, I'd find a way of getting it . . ."

Seeing an all too familiar argument about to begin, Saz jumped in.

"Actually, I expect she's straight and married, with no parents and she's exceedingly dull which is why a date with John Clark, secret jazz fiend, is her idea of excitement and that's why she chose such a stupid pseudonym. But isn't there some kind of missing persons file you could check for me?"

Helen vocalised an apology to Saz and stroked one on Judith's hand.

"All right, get us a physical description and approximate dates of disappearance and I'll see what I can come up with. I'll get someone to check any unidentified floaters too, but she's probably too recent to be any of the bodies they've had washed up in the past month."

"Thanks Hell. I'd rather she wasn't dead really. She's got me interested, I really want to know why she chose the months . . . and what she did the rest of the weekend."

Helen burst out laughing.

"Sorry Saz, but that's what our argument's about. Judith's mother keeps asking me to 'come down' for the weekend – you know, the whole middle-class happy family at the country 'cottage' bit, but I've told Jude I won't go as a flatmate, only as her lover."

"And that my darling, is impossible. Because a) we're not middle class, we're upper middle and b) in the case of you coming home as my lover she wouldn't let me in the house either. Actually she probably wouldn't let me within a six mile radius of anyone from the Townswomen's Guild."

"Aren't there any dyke Townswomen?"

"What's a Townswoman?"

"It doesn't matter Saz. Just Helen's way of deflecting the conversation back to our own problems."

"She might be fine. She's always very nice when I speak to her on the phone."

"Helen! Leave it. You don't know my mother. She's very nice to the rubbish collecting man too – but she wouldn't want him sharing my bed either. Anyway, it helps Saz not at all to know that her April or May might or might not be off to the country for the weekend after a night out on the town with this John bloke."

"No. But I bet his parents know what his sexuality is!" called Helen over her shoulder as she picked up the glasses for another trip to the bar leaving Saz with Judith.

"God knows why I love that woman. Well anyway Saz, why don't I check out John Clark for you? Big sister is everywhere and I'm sure I could get some info from British Telecom, I can certainly find out if he's got any sort of nasty record."

"Are there nice ones?" Saz looked up from her fresh gin and tonic.

"Yeah, Madonna sings country with k.d.lang. No, stuff like soft drugs aren't going to be of much interest in conjunction with Miss Months of the Year. But blackmail, or fraud, or any tacky sex stuff really . . . could be helpful. Yes, indeedy, Detective Chief Inspector here I come!"

Judith gleefully rubbed her hands together.

"This is absolutely why I became a policewoman – Trixie Belden, Nancy Drew. . ."

"Helen Mirren! Don't worry Saz, end of the week we'll have it all for you. In fact, come over for lunch on Sunday, after all Judith will be keeping the home fires burning, so perhaps you'd like to keep me warm? I mean we could . . . aaagh!"

Helen sprang up as Judith tossed a handful of ice cubes down her front, spilling two half eaten packets of crisps and all of Saz's drink, mostly over Helen.

Saz took that as an indication that if she stayed any longer it would soon end in tears and that if she drank any more her morning run would be an agonizing experience. She made her goodbyes, agreed to meet Helen in the coming weekend and squeezed through the mass of bodies to go home. Alone. And happy.

CHAPTER 7

Price fixe

Neither of us had ever lived with anyone before. As in "living with" – de facto, common law, live-in-lover. Wife. We'd both fought it off because of the obvious lack of freedom, the lack of "self-time" scared us. Had been sacred to each of us. Because of the commitment and because no one had ever wanted us to live with them. But five months into our relationship it became inevitable. Inexorable, like death. Dolores professed to be glad for me but I could tell she was sceptical. It wasn't just my feminine intuition – she told me so.

"I don't mind you moving out Maggie, really I don't. I think it's very . . . healthy. And I'm really happy for you, for both of you, but you know . . . if you ever want to come back, if you ever want to come grovelling back, if you ever need to drag your small and devastated ounces of pride back here . . . there's always the spare room."

"Or the other half of your bed Dolores? Listen sweetheart, even if it didn't work out. I wouldn't want to live with five people again. With five 'wimmin' again. With five women, two dogs, six cats, a host of ex-lovers and a dozen or so assorted therapies. I'm moving on Dolly, moving forwards, I don't want to live in the Moosewood Cookbook any more."

"Yeah, well, thanks very much. No, no it's fine, leave Susie Fat Cat with me, desert us all – only don't come to me for a quick snack on Yom Kippur."

I think Dolores was most pissed off, not because I was leaving our co-dependant rabbit warren of a communal household, but because I was moving in with another Jewish woman. It had always pleased her, appeased her, to think that she and I could never have worked out because of some inherent anti-semitism flowing in my Catholic veins. As long as Dolores could convince herself that we were not suited because I couldn't cope with her (adopted) cultural heritage and her (just discovered) collective unconscious, she could ignore the fact that our relationship hadn't worked simply because Dolores was mad. And she never did the dishes.

We searched for somewhere to live for most of February. Cold, grey, rainy, windy February. Cheap squalid flat after expensive palatial apartment. She of course, had a "proper job" and therefore much more money than me, always had, and so had no idea that ugly could be made beautiful with a tin of matt vinyl magnolia and a couple of tons of carpet cleaner. She wanted *House and Garden* and she wanted it now!

She wants everything "now". Maybe she has it.

Finally we found it – through a friend of a friend's ex-lover; naturally. Two floors up, halfway down a hill, with panoramic views of the Thames – through binoculars (and only in autumn and winter – the other seasons meant that the leaves on the huge green oak obscured all views except those of the dogs pissing against the trunk). Nice place, light and airy and completely empty. Open for us to put whatever mark on it we would. Furniture shopping was hard – she wanted "Little House on the Prairie" and I wanted "The Starship Enterprise". We compromised and ended up with the inside of a genie's bottle (harem red and gold with half of Kew in the window boxes) in the lounge and virginal simplicity in the bedroom. I painted, she called me on the phone three times an hour and we moved house in March.

It was then the shit with her family really hit the fan.

"I'll kill her" – her father.

"My poor baby" – her mother.

"Don't you touch my children" – her sister.

"What are you paying that therapist for?" – her brother-in-law.

"You've made a fool of me" – her father.

"How could you move so far away?" – her cousin.

"But what about the family?" – her mother.

Yes indeed, what about the family? So loving, so close, that when she'd come out four years earlier they'd decided it was a phase and ignored her. Well no, ignored IT. Still spoke to her – just not about the thing that mattered. She was twenty-eight at the time. Obviously too young to know her own mind. This loving close family that refused to accept their daughter in reality. This loving, cloying family that thought she was sick. But most of the venom they reserved for me, the big mean nasty dyke who'd contaminated their baby and brainwashed her.

"She's after your money."

"She's using you."

"She's taking advantage of you."

I never had that much power over her. Not even when I wanted to. She always did exactly what she wanted. Always.

Until now.

They refused to meet me or hear my name mentioned. It spoilt their closeness to let an outsider in. When her older sister had married, the husband didn't quite take her name, but he might as well have. He got a job in the father's firm, a company car and they rented a house from the cousins who were in real estate. I believe the idea was "not losing a daughter, but gaining a business partner". I, on the other hand, could hardly go to work in the family business – not a lot of call for a vegetarian shiksa in kosher butchering.

Butchering.

We lived together but she went to see them every Friday, occasionally she'd even stay the night, it made me furious that she'd trot along to see these people who despised me. I felt betrayed and consulted my Jewish friends.

Esther said it was inevitable.

"They're old, they're Jewish, you're a woman, you're a shiksa for God's sake! What do you want, enlightenment from grandparents? I'm sure her friends are right – they're probably lovely people, she's probably right to love them, they just can't cope with this one thing – well these two things really, you are Catholic after all. It just goes against everything they've ever believed in. Everything they hoped for her. You can't hate them for being just as bigoted as at least three quarters of the population. Give them time. It probably won't make any difference, but at least you'll get used to it."

She was wrong. I never did get used to being hated by strangers.

I went to Dolores who told me it was anti-semitic to think that Jews couldn't be as aware as anyone else. It was

Catch 22 and I was well and truly caught. Courted and caught.

I'm free now.

The Woman with the Kelly McGillis Body said she loved them, they were her family, she promised she'd never let them separate us and anyway they'd be sure to come round in time.

A month is time. So is a decade. So is a century. How long did she think I'd wait?

Her mother rang yesterday. I listened as she left a message on the answerphone.

"Darling, it's Mummy. I'm worried about you. We haven't seen you for weeks. Are you all right? Please call me."

Weeks! I last spoke to my father four months ago. I last spoke to my mother in 1986, two months before she died. Her mother never asks about me. I think it would make her sick to say my name. I wiped the message off the tape. What kind of a grown woman calls herself "mummy"?

The first three months were the worst. Our rough edges ripped the soft underbelly of the cosy coupledom we were hoping for. We had to rub hard against each other to sand the edges down. But while we were still raw we had the best sex.

It was so hard getting used to each other. She had different sleeping patterns – bed at midnight, up at 8.30am. I learnt to get up with her, make her tea, kiss her goodbye and then go back to sleep. I cooked for her, made her packed lunches, had a cup of tea ready for her when she came home. I took care of her. She got sick and I made her chicken soup. Real chicken. I found myself becoming her wife without any sign of a proposal. I'd never lived with just one person before. She'd never lived with anyone but her family and then eight years living alone. She learnt to eat regularly. To bathe by candlelight – I can't stand bright light in the bathroom. She learnt to love 60s comedy programmes. I read the Haggadah. We had sex every-where. The kitchen, the big sitting-room – filled with her books, thirty-six boxes of books carried up three flights of stairs. Mostly by me – she was never very strong. Made love in the tiny hallway – me pushed up against the door of the linen cupboard, forced against the door of the linen cupboard. In the bathroom, hot from my bath and getting so sweaty and wet I had to plunge straight back in again. And making love in our bedroom, with its sloping attic roof and the very tip of the Canary Wharf Tower just visible above the oak. Red light blinking at us. Winking at us. Phallic at us. We made love daily. Twice daily. Thrice daily. I went to work sore from sex and glad of it.

And then the ecstasy wore off and we settled down to Real Life. She worked days, I worked nights, we kept weekends and occasional free nights sacred for each other. At first she went out visiting her friends when I was working, but I didn't like it when she came home later than me. She arranged to meet them at lunchtimes. Occasionally her work took her out of London for a couple of days and she still saw her family three Fridays a month, but saved one for me. Sometimes she even slept over at their house, in her old childish single bed. But every other day I was there at six when she came home from work and she was there when I came home late. I loved to know she'd be there waiting for me. I loved the security of knowing she'd always be there.

Always be here.

She wasn't as tidy as me. But she learnt.
I wasn't as clean as her. But I learnt.
I cooked mostly. She ate and loved my food. I ate and loved
her body. I adored her legs. She adored how I ironed her T-
shirts. I wore her clothes. She never wore mine. I gave her
a stuffed toy. An elephant. She never named it and it
became Ellie to both of us. We took Ellie on his first Gay
Pride march. It was her first march too. Her first march of
any kind. She educated herself in politics and I educated
myself in Jewish festival lore. At New Year she went to her
family for the first night and we had friends over for the
second. Nuts and honey cake to start, spicy Mexican food
to follow. At Passover I learnt to cook with matzo meal. At
Yom Kippur I went hungry and thirsty. Dolores relented
and said,
    "So I was wrong. So her family hate you and she still
loves you. As Grandma Bernstein said 'Never kill a
chicken until you've counted its feathers' – loses a bit in
translation huh? I'm sure it meant something appropriate
in Yiddish."

As I said, Dolores only met her grandmother those few
times.

We lived together as wife and wife for three years. It was
happy and fulfilling and then I found out stuff. Stuff I
couldn't have imagined. I never lied to her. I never lied. I
was always completely honest. But she told me fibs and I
found out.

I hate lies.

CHAPTER 8

No pain, no gain

Saz woke up feeling uneasy. Why? What was she doing today that would require less than a jubilant greeting of a new grey afternoon? It took her a while to get the clear thought in her head, but when it came it dawned like January over London – cold, dreary and no hope of Christmas to enliven the proceedings. She was having lunch with Caroline. Caroline her ex-lover. Caroline the reason she had vowed to remain celibate for at least two lifetimes. Caroline with the delicate thin body, the deep green eyes, the tiny pale lips, the fine cheekbones. Caroline with the new Australian lover.

Saz and Caroline had been together for eighteen months when, one Saturday morning as they lay in bed, Caroline said she had "something difficult to say". Saz felt the cold hand of terror grip her stomach and waited for Carrie to explain why she hadn't wanted to make love, the first thing they did every morning. She lay passive and listening as Caroline said the traditional:

"I'm sorry, I love you, you're wonderful, it's not your fault . . . believe me, I'm sorry but . . ."

But she'd met someone else.

But she'd only known her for ten days.

But it was enough.

But she had to do what she had to do.
But she never meant to hurt Saz.
But she had to be true to herself.
But they could still be friends.

They parted two days later. Caroline promising to stay
in touch and Saz promising herself holidays, bottles
of gin, free and easy sexual liaisons, lots of parties,
something, anything . . . just stay sane. Saz called
Caroline several times in the next month but Caroline
was always too busy to talk for long. Finally a letter
came saying she was sorry, but perhaps it would be for
the best if Saz didn't call anymore, a clean break and all
that . . .

And now here it was eleven months since that letter and
Caroline, knowing her habits, had managed to catch Saz
just at her most vulnerable – the moment when she came
in from her run, just before she turned the answerphone on
as she was about to go back to bed.

"Hello?"
    "Ah, Saz, it's Caroline . . . um, hello. How are you?"
    "Stunned."
    "Yeah, well look, um . . . I know it's been ages, and I
know I said you shouldn't contact me . . ."
    "I didn't, the phone rang this end. You called me."
    "Yeah. Um . . . Saz, I'd like to see you."
    "Why?"
    "Well, because I'm moving to New York in two days
time. For good. I'd like to see you before I go."
    "New York? Not Australia?"
    "No. Not Australia. Look could we have lunch or some-
thing? I would like to see you."

And, like the stupid, forgetful, easily swayed idiot she was, Saz had agreed. What's more she'd invited Caroline to her flat. In sixty-five minutes time.

She got out of bed, dusted, vacuumed, washed, dressed (in the most stunning, just-thrown-on effect she could manage), dashed down to the shop to buy flowers (to herself, from herself) and waited. Waited for over half an hour because, as always, Caroline was thirty-five minutes late.

Caroline arrived with apologies and a bunch of flowers – same as the bunch Saz had bought an hour earlier, same shop, same price, different intention. Not "see how happy I am", but "see how sorry I am". She stood on the doorstep looking like it was this time two years ago.

Saz caught her breath and asked her in.

Caroline sat at the kitchen table, drinking weak coffee, looking thin and pale and beautiful with her fine, straight, auburn hair falling over her face. Caroline sat at the kitchen table and told Saz all about it. How the Australian had cheated on her, lied to her, used the car and flat for six months and then gone back to Sydney leaving only a huge phone bill and a postcard saying "Thanks for the hospitality but my visa's run out." How Caroline had wanted for months to run back to Saz begging forgiveness and kisses. How she'd stayed away until she could trust herself to behave sensibly. How she didn't want Saz back, not that she assumed Saz wanted her, how she knew she needed to be alone. Which was why she was leaving to go to film school. In New York. The money was coming from her dad who probably hoped she'd find herself a nice American boy. And now, well now she needed to say goodbye. And sorry. Properly.

Saz sat listening spellbound. She really did look very thin. And her skin. She'd forgotten that Caroline didn't have very good skin. Not enough exercise. She'd also forgotten what wonderful eyes she had. And her hair. The way it fell over her eyes. The way Caroline flicked it back without even a pause in the conversation. The way she wanted to kiss her. Caroline talked so long and so hard, telling her story so fully Saz wondered if maybe she'd given up therapy. She hadn't. She just wanted Saz to understand.

"Yeah Carrie, I know, I do understand. I understand that what you do is run away. I understand that we were becoming too close. I understand that you want me to forgive you so you can go off to New York feeling whole and happy and clear. I understand that going to New York is just running away again. I understand that this is the third career-oriented course you will have done in five years. I mean how long have you wanted to be a film-maker? What happened to furniture design? I understand that it's easy for you to keep running away as long as your father keeps funding you. I understand that as long as you let your father fund you, he will never treat you like the adult you want him to. I understand that now you know what it feels like to be left. And while I must admit I'm sorry for you, I'm also glad. I understand Caroline, that even at twenty-four it's about time you grew up. Perhaps it's a good move. Do you think you can stick at this one?"

"I don't know. But I want to try. I don't want to fuck up again. I'm sorry you're still so pissed off at me . . ."

"Only because you wouldn't let me be pissed off at you six months ago. If you'd have let me shout at you last year I'd be fine now and shagging half of North London."

"North London? I thought you'd want to stick to this half of the river after me."

"Anyway I'm not pissed off at you. And I'm celibate. And I'm bitter. I'm a bitter, twisted old dyke. Obviously."

Saz laughed despite herself as she quoted Caroline's mother, who when Caroline had come out had accused her daughter, aged fourteen, of being a "bitter, twisted old dyke". She'd then apologised and been sweetness and light ever since, but it was a big accusation for Caroline who, at fourteen thought she knew everything and now at twenty-four was just beginning to admit that she still wasn't quite "grown-up". The laughing helped. Saz told Caroline that she thought she'd been an absolute bitch and deserved everything the Australian had done to her. Caroline agreed though she thought the phone bill for £368 was a bit much and made more coffee. They asked about each others' families, mutual friends who had split off on either side and other friends who had never been mutual.

They ate lunch. Caroline as always ate lots though she looked like she ate nothing. They listened to Tracy Chapman and Kate Bush for old times' sake. By 4pm they knew all about the past year of each others' lives and Caroline had to leave. She left leaving an address in New York – luck being what it was for Carrie she'd been given a flat in New York in exchange for her London flat – minimum six months, possibility of two years – and the offer to Saz of a sofabed whenever she wanted it.

Saz closed the door behind Caroline and sighed. The phone rang. It was Gary.
  "I've got the names of two hundred women, physical descriptions – height, weight, hair and eye colour. I've even got marital status and occupation where available."

"Gary, brilliant! You're an angel, what do I owe you?"

"Two tickets to 'As You Like It' at the Barbican?"

"Sure sweetheart, when do we go?"

"Ah. Well actually, I'd really just like the tickets if you don't mind. I've got someone I'd like to take."

"Gary! You've got a date?"

"Yes and no questions or you don't get the info. You book the tickets, I'll send the papers."

"It's a deal. But she'd better be cute!"

Saz did the dishes and made a mental note to call Helen or Judith as soon as she was finished cleaning up. She wanted to get cross-referencing as soon as possible.

The phone rang again just as she was putting away the last cup. It was John Clark.

"John. Any progress for me?"

"Well Ms Martin, I've typed out a full physical description, a list of all of the restaurants we ever went to, I've got the date of when she broke her ankle and, I don't know if this will be of any use to you but I've got a postcard she sent me . . ."

"A postcard?"

"Yes, she sometimes went on business trips midweek – once though, it overlapped our dinner night. So she sent a postcard to my work instead."

"Where's it from?"

"New York."

"New York! Any address?"

"Well just a hotel address . . ."

"John that's brilliant! Don't you see? She'll have to have given the hotel some name and address for London!"

"Oh yes, of course, I didn't think . . . shall I call the hotel?"

"No, there's no way they'd give that information over

the phone. Just get all your info to me and I'll see what I can do. I was thinking of taking a quick transatlantic trip anyway . . ."

Saz hung up having arranged to meet John the next day.

Then she picked up the phone to tell Caroline the good news.

CHAPTER 9

Leftovers

After a while of living together it became obvious I'd have to meet more of her past. And as I couldn't meet her family then it would have to be friends. And ex-lovers. I hate meeting ex-lovers. I hate the history that they hold. We both have ex-lovers who are men. Mine are an eclectic collection of performers and artists, men I knew at university, old flatmates, present lovers of other friends – about one third of them gay. Some of them were gay when we met, some weren't. It took me a long time to make up my mind too.

The Woman with the Kelly McGillis body only has a few ex-lovers. She has three women and three men. Her men are a different sort of men to mine, mine are much more like boys. Hers are a doctor, a lawyer and a carpenter. Men to take home to mother. When we first met she couldn't get over the number of ex-lovers I have, male and female.

"But Maggie, how did you fit them all in?"

I chose to avoid the obvious joke. I can be quite ruthless when it comes to comedy.

"Look honey, most of them are friends – we were friends, we became lovers and then we went back to being friends again. If you don't have to spend the first three months just getting to know each other and if you don't have to stay together just because otherwise you'll never see each other again – then you can get through an awful lot of lovers. Besides that, it's kind of nice, like keeping it in the family."

I felt strange about all her relationships. I didn't want to know about them and yet I did. I'd ask about them and then when she told me I'd get angry and jealous. I'd try to hide it but I'm not very good at hiding.

I suffer terribly from jealousy.

I met one of the men once. The carpenter. He seemed nice. And completely innocuous. Dull. Which annoyed me even more. Because if he was so dull and so nice, how was it that she'd ended up with me? That she said she wanted to spend forever with me? Was there in me some hidden shred of boring which she found attractive?

Though there is something about boring which is attractive. A life with no surprises. A life with no change.
   I don't like change.

We went to dinner at the carpenter's house. He'd just finished renovating it. It had taken him five years. And he'd enjoyed doing it. Enjoyed stripping the banisters by hand. Enjoyed sanding the skirting boards, replacing the sashes on the old windows. I'd have ripped it all out and replaced it with chrome. Something clean and crisp with no hidden recesses. So nothing can hide away.

It did look wonderful, but he said there was still damp in the walls and rot in the foundations. He told us about the rot as if that wouldn't shatter the view of all that we'd just seen.

Once I know that something's rotten, I can't see it any other way.

And then when she went upstairs to the toilet he told me that he liked me. He liked me and he wanted to have sex with me.

I must have looked stunned because he said it again.

"I mean it Maggie, I think you're really beautiful. You're driving me crazy."

Even if I'd wanted to, that would have done it. I couldn't possibly have sex with someone who says "driving me crazy".

"No Peter. I couldn't. Apart from anything else, I couldn't do it to her."

"Well, we can have a threesome."

Then I knew he was a bastard.

"No Peter. We could not have a threesome. Not only would it bore me senseless, but she wouldn't like it. She doesn't have good sex with men."

"But she told me . . ."

"She was twenty-two, Peter. At that age women often lie to men. Some women do it all their lives. Some women really believe it would harm a man irreparably to hear that they were an incompetent lover."

He was blustering now, "I'm not . . ."

"How do you know? Can you be sure that not one of the women you've seduced with your masterful technique was faking it?"

"Well no, but you just know don't you?"

"Do you Peter? Do you know what it feels like to be a woman? Do you know what good sex feels like for a woman? I know because I'm a woman. How can you possibly?"

He was deflating in front of me. And the more I pushed home my point, the further he moved away from me. Not that it's even a point I believe in. There's a big myth surrounding "women-loving-women", it sells a lot of books. No one can ever really know how another person feels. But it's a great argument when dealing with a Neanderthal.

Then the Woman with the Kelly McGillis body swayed her slightly drunken way back down the stairs and came to sit beside me. Holding my hand and occasionally kissing my bare left shoulder. And we talked of nothing for another hour or so until she and I left for home. She was getting into the car as I turned to say goodbye to him on the doorstep. I looked up at him and was momentarily shocked to see that Mr Dull-and-Boring was long gone. He grabbed my wrist very tightly and snarled "You're wrong, she did enjoy it. She never faked a thing."

But it was him that was wrong there. She might have had good sex with him. Her memories, what she told me of its mediocrity, may have changed with the mists of time. But she did fake things. Lots of things.

We went home, car windows wide open to the cool air and made love slowly, desultorily. I took a long time to come and when I did it was fitful and barely satisfying. And again I marvelled at how such a stunning woman could have liked, even loved, a man so bland.

Until I remembered how tightly he grabbed my wrist and the look on his face as he stood in the doorway and I realised that perhaps she'd seen that look, that anger before too. Perhaps she liked it.

I think maybe she did.

Only one of the women lovers was a problem. She wanted to be my friend. I didn't even want to know her.

Victoria Cook was an artist.

I expect she still is, but we don't send Christmas cards.

She was a painter who exhibited at small, primarily women-only galleries. And after we'd been together for about a year and a half, Victoria Cook decided she wanted to be our friend. My friend.

Dolores knew her through a women artists' group she used to go to. She thinks she's weird. And if Dolores thinks Victoria is weird then she's got to be strange. However she, and most of the rest of the world also think Victoria Cook is very, very beautiful. Cool, charming, tall and gracious. All the things I always wanted to be and never became, being too short and loud and "cute". Cute is good, but it's not gracious. And unfortunately Victoria isn't one of those women who avoid their ex-lovers at all costs. She "maintains relationships". She takes her problems to her therapist and uncovers a "difficulty-strategy". After staying away for quite some time Victoria realised that she had a difficulty with me being the new lover and came up with a strategy that involved me becoming her new friend.

I'd rather appreciated her staying away. They say it's better the devil you know, but I prefer my devils snuggled up with the skeletons in the closet where they belong.

Victoria wanted to come to terms with me. Which meant she got to share her tales of life with the Woman with the Kelly McGillis body. She got to give me their history, when I liked to think there was no past before me. Victoria invited us both for lunch twice and drinks once. I went, each time feeling like I was late for the execution of my own relationship. They'd been together for just seven months and much of that time Victoria had been "developing an installation" so they'd only been able to see each other once or twice a week.

"And you know Margaret, I never felt I really had a handle on her. Always felt there was something else going on."

I always want to hit people who call me "Margaret".

"Well, you were busy with your work Victoria."

"Yes, but I always felt she was not quite as committed as I was."

That lack of commitment had caused Victoria to end the relationship with a terse note asking for no contact for six months.

"To give me time to see reality."

Within those six months the Woman with the Kelly McGillis body had met me and I'd become her reality. We saw Victoria three times and each time led to huge arguments between us.

"Look Maggie, she only wants to get to know you. Can't you humour her?"

"It doesn't humour me to think of you being with her. Where's the comedy in that?"

"It was years ago, I'm with you now. I want to be with you. For God's sake, I've been with you longer than I've ever been with anyone!"

The more I heard about Victoria, the more insecure I
became. I know jealousy isn't attractive but there's
nothing like wishing it away to make it even stronger.

Wishes are for the tooth fairy.

When Victoria realised I wouldn't play along in the way
her therapist would have preferred, she sort of dropped
away from our life. Slowly, like the scab coming off a particularly nasty sore. I don't know if the Woman with the
Kelly McGillis body missed her or not. But after all, she
did have me, and I'm enough for any woman.

Or should be.

And the fourth woman lover was me.
    Still is.

CHAPTER 10

The New York Marathon

New York was cold. Cold in that special New York way. That is, colder in temperature than London, but the friction of living there making it seem about nine times as hot.

Saz arrived late on Friday night and spent the weekend with Caroline, ice skating in Central Park, queuing outside in a virtual blizzard for tickets to a modern operetta at La Mama. They drank lots of espresso, ate too many doughnuts and even more bagels and then Saz spent Sunday afternoon alone in the Guggenheim, walking round and round trying to decide the best way to approach the hotel.

The information she'd gained in the week while waiting to go to New York had hardly been groundbreaking. "September" had stayed in a small private hotel on West 43rd and John Clark remembered her once saying that she always stayed in the same place when she went to New York. Which sounded like she went there often. She had told him that it was almost always midweek, though occasionally it had been one of the Fridays when she wasn't with him. Gary's information had been even less helpful and more time consuming. Having gone through every one of the two hundred names he'd given her, getting physical descriptions of the deceased from wherever she could –

workplaces, colleges, school records – she got the list down to sixty white women of about the right height and weight. She then cut it down to only twenty women with brown eyes and blonde, fair or dyed blonde hair. And then the hard part came. Using the details Gary had given her, she contacted the relatives where they were listed and began the agonizing job of trying to get a photograph of the deceased from each of the grieving relatives. In most cases she pretended to be an old school friend who'd read the death notice and was devastated not to be able to make it to the funeral. Could they bear to spare her a photo of Julie/Sally/Diane, just for a few hours so she could go and get a colour photocopy made? The families were usually helpful and friendly, adding to Saz's guilt even more. Where they were difficult she did more checking to get a photo from school magazines or office security departments. Finally she had photos of eighteen of the women and when John Clark had gone through them about five times and still said that none of them were September, Saz got Judith to take him to the morgue to see if he could identify either of the two unnamed blondes lying cold and unburied after four weeks. He couldn't.

"So, John, none of these brown eyed blondes are September. Now that could mean several things. To be blunt, perhaps she died somewhere else, and though you may find this difficult to believe, I don't have access to all the death records in the world. But what I think is much more likely is that she really did rip you off, she took your money and. . ."

"She wouldn't do that."

"How can you be so sure?"

"I know her . . ."

"You don't even know her name!"

"We know that! Hear me out. It's true I don't know her

name, but I know her. She wouldn't cheat me. She's in trouble and I still want you to find her."

"Look John, I don't think you can afford this, you still don't have a job, to take it any further I'm going to have to go to New York. The air fare alone is two hundred quid."

"Go. Just go. She needs me."

John Clark looked like a man obsessed. Gone was the "Mr Grey" Saz had met weeks before, this man had a dream, it was to get September back, it was to have dinner every second Friday night, whether that proved to be the most expensive meal of his life or not.

So here she was, early Monday evening, outside a "private hotel". And she'd been outside this "hotel" for nearly an hour, consulting her map, looking frantically at her watch as if she was waiting for someone and watching the people go in and out. But mostly in. And mostly men. And all very well-dressed. Glad she'd thought to pack some "posh clothes", she finally decided to go in herself. She took off her coat to reveal a plain but well cut business woman's suit, slipped off her trainers and took her court shoes out of their plastic bag like any other New York yuppie and walked up to the desk with her finest Sloane voice.

"Um, excuse me, I wonder if you could help me?"

The desk clerk looked up, evidently surprised at the English accent on the chick he'd been eyeing through the door for the past half hour.

"Yes ma'am?"

"I'm afraid I was expecting to meet a Mr – ah, Mr Hannon. Patrick Hannon." Saz said, invoking her maternal grandfather as she always did in moments of stress.

"He said six thirty and I've been waiting outside for almost an hour and it's most dreadfully cold, so I wonder if you couldn't let me wait in here for just a moment. You do have a lounge?"

"I'm sorry ma'am, I don't know a Mr Hannon. He's a member?"

"A member? Oh. Well, I don't know. I'm terribly sorry, I'm only in town for a couple of days and he suggested we meet for a drink, I thought this must be a hotel he frequents . . ."

"No, ma'am. This isn't a hotel. It's a casino. But if you'll just wait up a minute I'll get someone to cover for me, and then I can go on up to March to see if maybe he's in the new members' lounge."

"I'm sorry . . . did you say March?"

"Yeah, I know it's silly honey, but we've got twelve rooms – one for each game, you know, and each one's named after a month, like blackjack's in October, roulette's in January, poker's in July . . . and there's one room which is just kind of a lounge. That's March."

"Well, what a . . . what an interesting idea. But look, I don't want to disturb you any longer and to tell the truth, Mr Hannon is my ex-husband, so if he can't be bothered to turn up on time, well, I'm sure I've got better things to do with my time than to sit around waiting for him!"

"That's the spirit sweetheart!"

By now the desk clerk was all but kissing Saz's feet so she decided to push her luck just that little bit further.

"So um, how does one join this club?"

"One is invited," came a cold voice behind her. Saz turned to see a tall, immaculately dressed man standing in front of her, on either arm was a beautiful woman, both with the darkest brown eyes – and though one of the women was black, they also both had the same long, blonde hair.

"Charlie, what's this lady doing here?"

"She was just waiting for someone, Sir. A Mr Hannon."

"And I presume you told her we had no Mr Hannons here?"

"Well, I was just going to check in the new members' lounge, sir. . ."

"No need, we have no Mr Hannon."

"Yes Mr James. Sorry Sir."

"Perhaps you'd like to call the lady a cab now Charlie and get back to work?"

"Yes Sir, right away Sir."

Charlie picked up the phone and Saz watched as Mr James and the two women, without another glance at her, swept out of the foyer and up the staircase. She turned to Charlie and hoping that his fear of his boss wasn't greater than his attraction to her, said "Don't worry about the cab Charlie, I have a car. But let me just give you this . . ."

Saz grabbed two of the cards at his elbow, scribbled Caroline's number on one of them and kept the other one hidden in her palm.

"I'm staying with a friend. You might like to call me and maybe we could meet? I don't know that many people in New York and it does get kind of dull . . . especially as my friend works days . . ."

She placed the card slowly in front of him, smiled her most provocative smile and slowly walked out of the front door, all the while praising her mother for her tuition in decidedly politically unsound flirting. Once safely away from the front of the building, she changed her shoes and began to run. Only when she was back in the subway on the way to the apartment did she turn the card over.

CALENDAR GIRLS
– Private Hotel –
We cater for your every need –
all year round.
MEMBERS ONLY

Saz let out a low whistle.

"Well, little Miss Goody Two Shoes September, what would John Clark have to say about this?"

That night she talked it over with Caroline as they fell asleep.

"I'm sorry Saz, but it sounds more like a brothel than a casino to me. Dolly bird blondes, rooms named after months . . ."

"But I saw men going in with women."

"There's some funny couples in New York!"

"I don't know. It didn't feel like a knocking shop. It looked quite passable – no flocked wallpaper anyway."

"It's not a knocking shop babe, it's a high class brothel. Or it could be drugs I 'spose."

"You think so?"

"Yeah, why not? A room for each 'drug of choice' as we Americans say."

"Carrie, you've been here three weeks."

"Columbus had only been here a day and he got to name the place."

"You could be right though, one of those girls, the one with the natural blonde hair did have really strange eyes. Her eyes were incredibly brown, massively dilated pupils."

"More likely her contact lenses than coke. Your Mr James isn't going to waste his merchandise on the staff – not while they're working anyway."

"What did you say?"

"I said he wouldn't waste good drugs . . ."

"No, not that. The contact lens thing."

"Well think about it Saz. If she's a natural blonde then the chances of her having brown eyes are pretty small. Not impossible but pretty small."

" 'O' Level biology darling, remember?"

And Saz did remember. Remembered John Clark telling her that September's eyes were so dark it was hard to tell what colour they were, that sometimes it looked as if her whole eye was taken up by the pupil. As Caroline's breathing became regular beside her, Saz silently kicked herself. Whether it was coke or contact lenses or both that had made September's eyes big and brown, it made her previous analysis of Gary's information redundant. It was also inevitable that Mr James knew something about it and the person who was most likely to be able to help her was Charlie. And she hoped her charm had more effect on him than on Caroline who was beginning to snore gently beside her.

CHAPTER 11

Cake but not candles

She'd been working as a tour guide. Not your ordinary "and this is St Paul's Cathedral" from the top of a bus, but a specialist guide. She'd take families out in her car, or if there were too many of them, a specially hired mini-bus. Usually day trips to some beautiful or historic part of Britain; Stonehenge, Bath, the Lakes. Mostly the customers were American, occasionally French or German. She knew a lot about most places, but if they had a special request she'd spend nights in the library, boning up on all the facts. Sometimes she'd stay with them longer, taking them on up to Edinburgh or down through to Paris, Amsterdam. When she had to stay away I was usually rewarded with a special bottle of wine or some good Dutch cheese. Mostly she brought back some kind of objet d'art too. Usually some ugly touristy thing her guests had bought her to remind her of their great time together. Luckily she managed to break or lose most of them within a couple of months. When she wasn't touring, and most tours were midweek, she'd go into her office to plan the next assignment or take future bookings. As I said, when I first heard about it, her job sounded terribly glamorous. In truth, she usually came home exhausted and wanting to sleep for a couple of days. Still, it paid the bills – all the bills, most of my share too. And it got her out of the house. I was hoping to get a surprise trip for my birthday, but it wasn't to be.

That's when I first found her out.

It was the third of my birthdays we'd shared but the first to fall on a Friday. It was not one of the Fridays per month I'd been allotted but I assumed she'd be with me anyway. I assumed wrong.

"What do you mean you're going to your parents?"

"I mean I'm going to my parents. I mean it's their night. It's one of their nights. I mean I ALWAYS go to my parents three Fridays a month. You know that."

"But it's my birthday."

"I'll take the day off work. I'll only go to them for a couple of hours. I'll meet you in town."

"No."

"I'll be home with you by nine thirty."

"No."

"OK. Well I'll bring dinner. I'll buy your favourite take-away. And we can have champagne. Well, you can have champagne. We'll get a video out. And we could go to a club. You know you always want to."

True. I did always want to go to clubs and she'd always promise to go with me and then discover she was too tired at about ten thirty.

"No. I want to be with you. It's my birthday for God's sake. I want you. What am I going to do by myself for four hours?"

"Oh, come on Maggie! You're a grown up, you've got friends, call someone, see if Dolores wants to go out and I'll come and meet you later."

"Right. Yes. Good move. That's ideal. Now ... what shall I say? – 'Hi, Dolly, it's Maggie. You know how you always told me it wouldn't work? Well it hasn't. It's my birthday and she's gone home to her mummy and daddy. And no they won't be sending me a present.' Now that would be the ideal present for Dolores wouldn't it? I can just see it, she'd be round here with open legs to comfort me in no time."

"There's no need to be crude, and anyway you know Dolores is far too much in love for that, even on your birthday!"

She was right. Dolores had fallen head over heels with a wonderful woman. A landscape gardener. And pagan. So now even my barbed confidante was not as free as she had been.

"You're right there. So what do you suggest I do? Sit at home and be the good little wifey until you're ready to come and play with me? Or perhaps I should come with you?"

That got her. She seemed genuinely scared that I should want to go with her. So scared in fact that it didn't occur to her that I couldn't possibly make the trek all the way to Golders Green merely to be insulted by her parents. So scared that she didn't even realise I wasn't serious. The protestations began.

"But you couldn't . . . I mean they wouldn't let you."

"They couldn't do much if I just turned up though, could they? Surely they wouldn't cause a scene in front of the neighbours?"

"Well, no they wouldn't. But you can't. It's not fair . . ."

"Not FAIR? It's MY birthday!"

"Well you can't, that's all there is to it. I won't take you."

"I'll go by myself. I'll just turn up and knock on the door. In fact I'll go early, before you've finished work, so I'm waiting there for you when you get there. I've got the address. Yes. That's it. I'll go by myself. About time I met the in-laws anyway."

I was furious by now, and so carried away that I almost believed I could do it. Almost believed I could brave their anger and hate. And she collapsed in front of me. Just collapsed like a punctured beach ball. Just curled up at my feet and begged me not to. Begged me not to go. Said she'd cancel. She'd stay with me. Said her mother couldn't cope. Said she was sorry. She was thoughtless. She hadn't known it mattered so much to me. Well, neither had I. She said she'd spend the whole day and night and every waking minute with me. Only she begged me not to go to her parent's house.

She begged me not to do it.

And because it was up to me, because I was in control, because it was my decision, I said I wouldn't.

"Don't be silly darling, of course I wouldn't go to your parents'. Can't think of anything less fun to do really. Anyway, now I come to think of it, Dolores said Annie was probably having a party that night so I think I'll go to that. You can come and get me later. I'd rather do that really anyway, after all, as you so rightly said, we do have the rest of our lives together."

She hated me for that. But she never could hate me for long. Because I can never hate anything for long and I don't let people around me stay mad. I get very, very angry, very quickly and then it's gone. Like it was never there, except for the burn marks where my white hot rage has scarred someone or something.

She looked scared – and scarred – for a day or two and then, when she realised I really wouldn't carry out the threat, life picked up as usual.

The way life usually does.

The day of my birthday dawned crisp and sunny with a strong breeze carrying promises of a clear day. I woke in her arms and, all pain of the previous week gone, began to make love for another year of my life.

Began to make love for another year with my love.

At nine thirty I rang in sick for her while she heated croissants and poured fresh coffee. We moved to the lounge for the sunshine and lay on pillows and duvet watching Susan Sarandon and Catherine Deneuve in *The Hunger* while we allayed ours. It was still early, before midday when she brought me clothes to dress in. Functional, warm clothes. Then she led me to the car where she blindfolded me and lay me in the back seat.

I got my day trip after all.

I succumbed to this order readily. For a treat with me as the centre I will always succumb.

It is when the event is not about me that I need to take control.

She drove, playing my favourite music for about two hours. My sense of time defined by which tapes were played and for how long. We arrived at the sea. It was sea by its sound and its smell. She sang to me in the back of the car and then she took me out to the shore. I taught her how to skim stones. To make them hop just across the surface of the water, to make them curve as if they could come back to you, just before they sink deep under. She told me the names of different kinds of seaweeds and we picked shells from their beds and told each other stories of the crabs that had lived there.

"This was Mr Joseph Crab. When his girlfriend told him she was pregnant he ran away to sea and became a . . . hermit crab!"

"This is Miss Caroline Crab, all the other crabs hated her because she was too big and ugly to fit into any of the old shells and her hands were always too hard and ungainly, then one day while looking in the Directory of Crabs and Crustaceans she discovered she was not a crab at all, but a beautiful baby lobster."

"So she climbed happily into a pot of boiling water and lived deliciously ever after."

"Maggie! That's so cruel!"

The Woman with the Kelly McGillis body wouldn't know. She eats bacon sandwiches but not shellfish or any seafood. Not so much dietary laws as allergies.

I'm allergic to very little. But when I am, it's obvious.

She brought lunch out from the boot of the car. Cheeses and bread, olives and hummus and salad and fruit and still frozen ice-cream and chocolate and champagne for me and beer for her. And so we ate and drank and feasted on each other and the day until it was mid afternoon and time to return. This time I watched as we drove home. Watched her sure and steady hands directing the car, much the same as her hands directed me. Sure, steady and always attaining their goal, my goal.

My hands are shaking.

She took me home where we washed and dressed. She for her parents, me for Maximum Impact. And then she dropped me off at Annie's house on the way to the house where she'd grown up.

I walked in, about three hours before most of the other party-goers. Annie and Dolores were upstairs. Dolores was dressing. I could tell by the shouts coming from the bedroom.

"No. NO. NO. NO. That's horrible. I hate them. I hate all my clothes. They're hideous. Horrendous. I hate them."

It was a cry I'd heard at least three times a week ever since I'd first known Dolores. Annie's brother let me in and took me into the kitchen for coffee. Annie and her brother run the landscaping business together. She came out when she was seventeen and went straight into gardening. He went to Oxford, married a very nice woman, was "something in the city", father to three children and the apple of his parents' eye. Then when he was forty-three his perfect wife died and he and the three teenage children, none of whom had ever done anything more domestic than make a cup of coffee, discovered they couldn't cope with grief AND housework. Annie moved her collective of housemates out and her family in. The five of them had lived very happily with each other and their fading grief for five years now, Keith doing the books and bookings and Annie doing the digging with occasional help from Keith's son. And now they had Dolores on semi-permanent loan from her grateful flatmates. Keith handed me coffee and I handed him a few bucketloads of sympathy.

"Honestly Maggie, it's not that I don't like her – how could I not? I love the woman. And the kids are besotted with her. Of course they are, she's completely loveable. It's just that she . . . well, I know she's your friend but she's . . . so. . ."

"Mad?"

"Yes. And she doesn't do the dishes."

"That's Dolly, Keith. She's also crap at getting dressed."

By the time Annie managed to force Dolores downstairs (wearing one of her dead grandmother's sequinned cock-tail dresses), other people were starting to arrive. The selection at Annie's parties was always eclectic. Though she was only recently with Dolores, we'd both known her for years, so a good deal of my past turned up at that party too. By about nine o'clock they were all there. Two of my ex-lovers, Keith's son and his girlfriend, his daughters and their boyfriends (it is a truth universally acknowledged, that given "alternative" parenting, teenagers will regu-larly emerge with partners far more suitable to their grandparents' choice than their parents'), Keith's mother, all of my ex-flatmates, half a dozen husband and wife couples and a gentle sprinkling of London lesbians. (The Brixton contingent stunning in mini skirts and platform shoes, the Stoke Newington crowd with DMs and dogs). And despite this huge group of people, loads of old friends, and a massive cake made by Dolores' own hands (no candles, but three incense sticks – that is reality for Dolores!), despite all this, I still wanted my darling. Wanted her to wish me Happy Birthday. Wanted her to sing to me. Wanted her to hold me. Wanted her.

Which is when I did it. Went to the phone. Picked it up. Dialled their number. And hung up straight away. Of course they wouldn't let me speak to her. Of course they'd hang up on me. So I grabbed Keith. I made him call them. A man asking for her wouldn't do anything but appease them. She'd thank me AND be able to talk to me. It was ideal.

Keith dialled to my instructions. He mouthed to me the phone was being answered. I could hear a man's voice. He asked for her. There was talking on the other end of the phone and then Keith said goodbye. He hung up.

"Um, I'm sorry Maggie. That was her father. He said she hadn't been there. Not all night. Not for a couple of weeks. He said to try her at home."

I called our home number, but of course there was no reply. I asked Keith not to mention it to anyone and sent him to get me another glass of wine. I went outside to sit and wait. And think. I didn't have to wait long. The car came round the corner within five minutes and I made my decision. It was my party and I didn't feel like crying. I wasn't prepared to argue with her so I decided not to mention it. Perhaps she'd been off buying my present. I ran inside to say goodbye and then dashed out to the car.

"Don't let's go back in. I just want to be with you. Let's go home now."
    "OK birthday girl, whatever you say."

On the drive home she told me about her evening. How her mother had asked about her job, how her father had just grunted when she bravely mentioned my name, how she'd stolen me another bottle of champagne from her parents' supply.

And I just smiled and nodded and accepted her story. Like I accepted her present – a beautiful, big oval silver and onyx ring. Accepted it even as I wondered how she could possibly afford it. She put it on my finger.

"Maggie, I'm sorry I couldn't be with you tonight. But believe me, I thought of you the whole time."

I let her kiss me and tried to return the kiss. I felt like my body was with her while my soul was off on the third level of Hell. I kissed her back then and held her very tight as if by holding her I could keep out the sharp splinter that was driving between us and cutting me. Cutting me up.

Of course I couldn't. Once it was in there, it had to drive much further in until it could be finally drawn out the other side and the wound cleaned to heal.

She stroked my hair for hours that night. Her last words before she fell asleep were "I want to stay with you for the rest of my life."

And she did.

CHAPTER 12

Dodgems

Saz didn't have to wait long for Charlie to come round. She was woken by the shrill alarm of a telephone call at 7am.

"Hey, ah, yeah . . . could I speak to Mrs Hannon please?"

"Mrs Wha . . . oh, yes, sorry, this is Mrs Hannon speaking."

Saz regained her accent and her composure.

"Is this Charlie?"

"Yeah, ah, you said I should call . . . I know it's early but I don't have a lotta time."

"No, of course not, Charlie it's fine. I did want you to call me. I'd like to meet you if I could. Soon. Today. Obviously, I've just woken up, but . . ."

"Well, why don't we meet for breakfast? I don't start again until three, so that should give us plenty of time."

Saz arranged to meet him at ten, hoping that five hours would be long enough – sure it was lots of time for what Charlie had in mind, but was it enough for her to get all she needed to know from Charlie?

She dressed in her most seductive outfit – mostly borrowed from Caroline and hailed a cab with the abandon brought on by spending a week in New York on John Clark's money.

She arrived at the coffee shop fifteen minutes early, wanting to be there before Charlie so she could set herself up with a nice high status position and give him lots of room to grovel to her. She ordered coffee for both of them and a croissant for herself. She didn't have to wait long for Charlie. He had obviously spruced himself up for the occasion. His shoes shone as brightly as his slicked back hair and he came armed with a small bunch of violets.

"For you, I hope you like them."

Saz felt almost guilty at having led him on so far, but decided to get on with her story anyway.

"Charlie, I'm afraid I must come clean about something straight away. I have to tell you I've deceived you."

His face fell, but Saz pushed on.

"You see Mr Hannon isn't my ex-husband. He's my present husband. And I want him back. That's why I've come to New York. To take him home."

Charlie looked more than a little pissed off, but when Saz started to cry, he obviously couldn't stay angry.

"Hey no, come on, don't cry. God, I hate it when a lady cries. Look honey, what can I do to help? I already told you we don't got a Mr Hannon at Calendar Girls."

"No. I know. I mean, obviously not. But let me tell you what I know. My husband has always been a gambler. Mostly in London, but occasionally, if we were on holiday he'd try other . . . establishments. Well, last time we were in New York was three years ago and I know he came to your workplace. He told me about it when we walked past one day. I think a business associate of his introduced him as a member."

"So who's that, perhaps this friend knows where he is?"

"The name is neither here nor there, Charlie. I probably

couldn't remember it if I tried. My husband knows so many people. Anyway, we have several businesses. Some are in my name and some in his and some in both of our mothers' maiden names. My husband is a very astute businessman, Charlie. He knows all about tax dodges. He could be a member of 'Calendar Girls' in any one of four or five names."

"But I don't understand . . ."

"Just listen and I'll explain. A few years ago, he started coming to New York more frequently. Usually midweek. Though I think there may have been a few occasions when he was here for a weekend, or at least a Friday night. Then, about two months ago it all came out – I found a long blonde hair on his jacket, confronted him about it and he told me."

Saz took a deep breath, a big gamble and started again.

"He'd met a girl at your club. He wasn't specific. I think she may have been English. Anyway he wanted to take her away from it all and . . . and I'm sorry Charlie . . ." Saz blew her nose and dabbed at her eyes.

"Well, we had a dreadful argument and then I suppose he must have taken her away, because I haven't seen him since. Which is why I'm here. Because I think if I can find her, then maybe I can find him."

Charlie reached for his coffee cup, finished his drink and looked up at her.

"You'd better be telling me the truth, because if you're not, we're both going to be in a lot of trouble."

"Why should we be in trouble? I'm only trying to find my husband."

"Let's just say Mr James doesn't like people to ask questions and leave it at that, yeah?"

"But can't you help me at all?"

"Look, all I can tell you is that there was an English girl who worked at Calendar Girls and she was a fine looking woman. As my granddad used to say 'Fine like a hot summer'. He thought of himself as a poet. He wasn't, he was a drunk. But anyway, that's why I called her June."

"June? That's her name? June?"

"No, Mrs Hannon. I don't know the names, any of 'em. It's like the gaming rooms, some of the girls are called by months of the year, some by days of the week."

"I see."

"So. This English girl. June. She didn't work regular. And not your midweek either. Well, hardly ever. Just one Friday night four or five times a year, but she was a looker and she was smart. So she didn't come to work a lot, but Mr James was real happy when she did, said no-one could get the money off them like she could."

"Get the money off them?"

"Sure, it's a gambling place, but you've got to get them to the tables first. Left to themselves, those guys would just talk business all night if they could. The girls get them to buy champagne. Dozens of bottles. Then they're drunk by the time they start to play – and the house can't lose. Well, hardly ever."

"So what happened to her?"

"I dunno. There was a big fight with Mr James and she went storming off. I guess she must have told him about your old man. Mr James doesn't like the girls to mix with the customers in that way – 'they start wasting their money on diamonds and pearls instead of diamonds and spades', that's what he says anyway. Yeah, it must be seven or eight weeks since I last saw her. Which fits in with your husband running off, doesn't it?"

"Do you think Mr James might know where she went?"

"Maybe. He was pretty fond of her. But you won't get him to tell you. He's very protective of the girls. That's why they all have the hair and the eyes."

"I noticed the two yesterday."

"They've all got it. It's weird sometimes, when you see fifteen or sixteen of 'em together. Just wigs, peroxide and contact lenses. We got white girls, black girls, Hispanics, Asians – and one or two of them natural. Only not many. It don't matter – they've all got the same hair and eyes. It's to 'protect them from the customers', Mr James says. But I reckon they look like the Stepford Wives when you get them all together. It's kinda creepy."

"Charlie, you've just given me a brilliant idea."

"What's that?"

"The Stepford Wives."

"Huh?"

"Well, I could do it. I'd only have to dye my hair."

"Oh no you couldn't, there's a lot more to it than just looking right. What do you know about gambling?"

"I could learn couldn't I? All the girls can't be pros when they start."

"You're too high class. You wouldn't know what to do if one of those rich old men started coming on to you."

"Oh really? I knew what to do with you didn't I?"

Charlie looked up sharply, then smiled.

"Well, I guess so. You got me there."

"Anyway, I'd only do it for a couple of nights. Just to get to talk to Mr James. Not even long enough to need to get good at it. Just to see if he knows anything about June. And my husband. Then I'll go back to London forever and no one will ever know the difference. Please Charlie, will you help me?"

"How?"

"You don't have to do anything. Just don't give me away when I turn up tomorrow looking for a job."

"What if James recognises you?"

"He won't, he barely glanced at me yesterday – he was much more worried about you giving away the trade secrets."

"I don't know . . ."

"Please?"

Saz took his hand and looked at him with all the imploring innocence she could muster thinking "Shit Saz, if this
doesn't work, you could always get a job as Lassie".

Charlie gave in. Saz bought him lunch and then left, armed
with the one ex-worker's real name that Charlie knew, a
girl he'd "spent a bit of time with" who was now happily
married in Ohio. The sort of friendly girl who could well
have given Calendar Girls' address to a good-looking
English woman travelling the States and looking for
work. Saz called Mr James and arranged an appointment
for the following day.

She then went back to Caroline's via the hairdresser.

"Hi Carrie, I'm home – and be thankful I've got naturally brown eyes."

CHAPTER 13

Brain food

I started going to the gym. And swimming. I thought about
starting to run but I couldn't afford the shoes. I started to
do all that "physical stuff" I'd scorned for years – Dolores
had once threatened to give up her softball team if I didn't
stop mocking it so much – I started it so that I could go out.
So I could be out of the house as much as possible. I
decided I had to cut her off before she could cut me out. I
thought I knew what she was up to and I needed to be one
step ahead of her. I started to work it out. It was quite nice
in a way – the gym was old, a bunch of machines in a
windowless, grimy room. Every night there'd be six or
seven of us there, no conversation, just sweaty grunting
and panting. It was like being in a boxing movie only
without the skipping. Best of all, I didn't have to talk to
anyone.

And I tried to get it clear in my head.
I'd work out and work it out.

The nights she'd spent away from home, not just evenings,
but whole nights – mostly Fridays, sometimes even
midweek. Nights away from our bed, nights away from my
body. Nights that she'd gone out straight from work and not
come back until the following evening. Never to friends, of
whom I could feasibly be jealous, always to her family.

"God, Maggie, just because they're being assholes, you can't expect me to divorce them!"

And I couldn't disagree with her. Family is family, and in Jewish households, like their pre-Vatican II counterparts, that's Family with a capital "F" – Dolores had taught me that much. But then, Dolores' family hardly count.

And then there were the several nights at a time, she'd been away on "business". No legitimate excuse for my complaint there either. I'd always known she had to go away for work sometimes.

I spent hours biking furiously on a stationary bike – counting up the nights we'd spent apart, not that many, six or seven a year at most – and after nearly four years that's not much. But then again, if they were twenty nights she'd spent with someone else, then yes it was "much" – far too much. And then there were all those Friday nights, ones where she'd come home late to me, but now I didn't know where she'd spent them. Certainly some of them must have been with her family – I don't suppose she went out and bought the honey cake she brought home to me, or the latke, carefully wrapped in greaseproof paper –

"I asked Mummy if I could bring something home."

"Did you tell her it was for me?"

"Not exactly, but she knows you're going to eat it too."

"That'll account for the unmistakable taste of arsenic then!"

"Unlikely, she knows I couldn't possibly give it all to you and not eat over half of it myself!"

We shared food late at night, food she'd brought to our home from wherever she'd spent the evening. We shared food and love and lust, crumbs in our bed, sheets on the kitchen table.

I eat alone now.

I'd swim another forty lengths, the whole time a litany of "Where were you?" going over and over in my head. All the nights I'd been out performing, nights I'd had no reason to call her at home, so now I'd never know if she'd been there or not. It was easy to cry in the pool – salt from my tears and chlorine in the water staining my eyes red.

My history was becoming untrustworthy – I now knew my recollection of events wasn't necessarily real. I couldn't trust my memory because my memory might be based on falsehood.

Perhaps she'd only lied to me on my birthday, on that one night.

Or perhaps she'd lied about them all.

And there was no one I could tell, no one I could share my pain with. Dolores liked her a little more, but not that much. Not enough to be OK about blatant lying. Besides Dolly was in love and her calls had dwindled to a mere one or two a week. She wouldn't understand and anyway I was too embarrassed to tell her. Too ashamed that this love of my life had turned out to be a dud like all the rest of them. Too ashamed to do anything other than let the pain fester and breed. I was furious and it just built up day after day, I fed it day after day. And I'd push myself to the gym, stomach churning with the strength of my anger, steel machines meeting the force of my rage.

I got pretty strong.

For a while we didn't see much of each other. She was still working days – out at nine thirty, home at six. If I had a gig

I'd be out of the house by eight at night. And I was trying much harder to get work – I had a stronger body and better bank balance than I'd ever had, only I felt like I'd lost the only person I wanted to share them with. The nights I didn't perform I'd mostly be at the gym or the pool. Sometimes both. I'd come home exhausted and fall into bed. And then there was our social life – occasional parties where we spent the night on either side of a crowded room – the modern ideal of a non-clingy twosome, dinners with the increasingly coupled Dolores and Annie.

For three months this went on. On the Friday nights that she'd "go to her parents" I would spend hours at the gym, sometimes not even working out, just waiting by the pay phone, trying to get up the courage to call her parents and ask if she was there. I didn't need courage to speak to her mother or father, I needed it to cope with what I might hear.

I never called them.

I've always sympathised most with the Lion in *The Wizard of Oz*. And not just because he has the best costume. A brain and a heart are all very well, but what are they worth if you don't have the courage to use them? And I hate the way Dorothy's pigtails turn into a mane of glossy auburn locks once she's in Oz. I'd have liked her better if she'd stayed the same.

I hate change.

So I couldn't call her parents. I didn't have the courage. I still haven't. Not even now.

But she knew something was wrong. I'm a good comedian, I'm not a good actor. And besides, she might have been lying to me, but she wasn't blind. Liars are probably the least blind people in the world, they have to watch all the time. Make sure, make ready, make believe.

I was shape changing. Building muscles and building hate.

It had to explode eventually.

One night she came home just as I was about to go out to the gym.

"Hi honey – I'm home!"

I used to love to hear those words, our life a parody of the happy all-American sitcom home. Now they just made me run faster.

"Hi babe. Look I've got to go, want to get to the pool before it closes. I might go to the gym too – I'll see you later."

"Oh not again Maggie. Couldn't you stay in with me just one night – please? It's been months since we just stayed in and did nothing together."

"I'm busy."

"You seem to be busy all the time these days sweetheart, what's going on – got another lover?"

"How dare you! You're . . ."

"Oh come on Mag, I'm only joking."

"Don't call me Mag."

"Give me a break! Can we talk please? Could you just tell me what all this is about?"

"I think you're the one who should be telling me don't you?"

"For God's sake babe, I don't know what you're talking about!"

"Liar!"

"What?"

"You heard. Liar! You're a fucking liar!"

I was crying now, twisting my gym shoes in my hands and crying. Big hot angry tears rolling down my face.

"Please Maggie, I don't know what you're talking about."

"My birthday. I'm talking about my bloody birthday."

"I don't . . ."

"You weren't there. I wanted to talk to you and you weren't there."

She knew she'd been caught. She looked like a rabbit in car headlights, like an employee with his hand in the till. She looked like anyone who knew they'd been found out. She looked scared.

"You called my parents?"

"Yes."

"Well . . . did you speak to my dad? You must have spoken to my dad, you know what he's like. He was probably lying. He probably knew it was you and didn't want you to speak to me."

I felt sick. I'd got her and she was lying even more. I answered her flatly.

"I didn't speak to him. Keith did. I got Keith to call so they wouldn't know it was me. So they couldn't lie."

"Oh."

"Your father told Keith you hadn't been there for a couple of weeks – which means you hadn't been there the Friday before either."

"No. I wasn't."

She guided me inside and shut the door. She took the shoe away from me.

I was crying even more now. Not just anger, now it was sorrow too. I felt deserted. She sat me down on the couch and stroked my hair. I wanted to pull away but I couldn't. I was too numb.

"Darling, I wish you'd have asked me about this ages ago."

And in a soothing voice she stroked my pain and put my worries away. She told me about the fight she'd had with her parents two weeks before my birthday. How she'd told them she couldn't be with them that night. It was the anniversary of her grandmother's death – they didn't understand that she could want to be anywhere else, that she could prefer to be with me. They didn't understand. And neither did I, none of us understood how torn she was, how she felt so ripped through her centre whenever the problems with her family and me flared up.

I curled up in her arms and listened as she spun a tale that wiped away my anger, as she told a story that calmed my heart. She told me about those Friday nights, how she'd spent the evenings in her car. On my birthday night she'd waited in the car until it was time to come to Dolores' party. Unable to be with me or give her family the satisfaction of giving in, she'd hidden, driven dark streets and thought of how much she loved me.

I listened as she placed a warm blanket over me and sent me to sleep. I listened as she pulled a warm blanket of wool over my eyes. I listened as she crooned me to sleep.
    "Oh my darling, I'm so sorry, you must have been so worried . . . it was only that night, well, those two . . . I didn't know what else to do, I couldn't make a decision about you or them, I had to run away . . . I'm sorry you've been so unhappy . . ."

She led me down a blind alley and I willingly followed. I was so desperately unhappy, so eager to be rid of my anger – so tired of going to the gym – that I let her twist me and tie me up.
    I let her feed me fables.

She came to me quiet that night. I was nearly asleep, worn out by all the emoting. Or maybe I was asleep but she stroked my shoulder and I turned to face her.

"No, don't move. Stay there. Lie there. Take off your shirt."

I took my T-shirt off and she lay on top of me, her breasts pressing into my shoulder blades, my almost sleeping body waking faster than my brain, warming to her lying on me. My body is a light sleeper. She pulled my arms out to the sides, gently turned my head so she could kiss me, slowly started to grind her pelvis, just below the small of my back, equal pressure, equal movements – her to me, me to the bed. She slipped her hands under me – one to my breast, one to my cunt. She kept up a steady rythm. My body was wide awake now. I was wide awake now – dragged back from sleep my body and myself were one, her body and myself seeming one. Both of us maintaining the rhythm, I started to cry out, her hand flew from my breast to my mouth.

"No sound."

"I can't not."

"Bite. Bite down."

Three of her fingers crammed in my mouth. I didn't bite. Couldn't bite the long delicate fingers that fed me. Sucked instead, warm and sweaty fingers in my mouth, in me. Rhythm still going, both of us in time, sweat in the small of my back sticking to her stomach. One backed beast we came together and fast. She slid beside me, grabbed handfuls of my hair and held me close.

"See? We couldn't do that if we didn't belong together. It wouldn't happen. You're mine and I'm yours."

Possession is nine tenths of the law.

But I believed her. Because it was easier to believe her. Because I had to believe her. Because if I couldn't believe in her, what was left for me to trust?

Nothing.

There is nothing left.

I have no faith anymore.

The nuns used to say that despair is the greatest sin. Judas was condemned not because he betrayed Jesus, but because, having betrayed, he despaired. Apparently God can forgive anything but despair. Clever God.

But I wasn't thinking about Judas then, the cock crowed thrice and I chose to believe. I made that leap of faith, I watched as she turned water into wine. I put all my eggs into the one basket and handed them over to her.

She makes a mean omelette.

CHAPTER 14

The Stepford races

Saz had already sold her ninth bottle of champagne by the time Mr James came in on Friday night – no mean feat for three hours of work with bottles of champagne selling for a minimum $200 a bottle. It was her second night and the first time that Mr James had come to check up on her. He'd employed her almost at once – apparently believing her story that she was a traveller who needed a bit of extra money before moving on again in a couple of weeks' time. He seemed to have no trouble believing that the woman from Ohio would have given Saz his address – said he often found his employees that way. Best of all he didn't seem to recognise her from Monday afternoon at all – though the fact that Saz's blue black bob was now pure peroxide probably had something to do with it. He said he liked her English accent, he loosened his soft silk tie, he didn't mind taking girls on for "holiday work", he asked her what she'd like to drink and told her that if she was any good at it he'd be happy to have her back next time she was in New York. Saz said she never drank at work, then he told her a few basic rules and left her to get on with it. It was simple. So far.

The other girls had shown her the ropes. How to talk to the New York businessmen like an intelligent bimbo – that is, always understanding what they were talking about, but never knowing more about it than them. How to spot the ones who wanted more than just champagne and cards – and how to fend them off politely. Finally and most importantly, though the least lucrative – how to deal with the ones who actually brought their wives or mistresses with them – act like a waitress.

Saz, well practised in lying and quick witted, took to it like a debutante to champagne. She'd been relieved when James had told her that he positively demanded a "friendly but celibate interaction between members and staff". And when she checked it out with the other staff she'd found that he actually meant it – a girl had been fired in the summer for having an affair with one of the members – and no, she didn't have an English accent. The rates of pay weren't great – a mere $90 for a six day week, or just $12 a day if you couldn't make all six – but then the tips were outrageous – one man had given her a $100 note for directing him to the bathroom, another gave her $50 for helping him on with his coat, and there was also a $20 commission to be made on each bottle of champagne sold. In two nights Saz had made over $600, what with that and the money owing from John Clark, she'd be able to afford half a dozen answerphones.

She was just starting to get into the swing of things, playing the gamblers off against each other, laughing at their unwillingness to buy more drinks when Mr James called her from the door,

"September, can I have a word?"

She'd frozen a little when he first said he thought she should be called September – she'd told him her name was Mary but he didn't want to check it out. He wasn't interested in references or the fake ID Saz had spent Wednesday arranging. "September" seemed a little too

close for comfort, but then she remembered it was only she
who'd called the missing woman September, Charlie had
called her June and of the five other girls she'd met, only
one remembered an Englishwoman and she had called her
April, "because she was English and England always
makes me think of spring – you know, like the Romantic
poets?"

Saz chose not to tell her about T.S. Eliot and the dead land
lilacs.

Actually, the other girls had been extraordinarily unhelp-
ful. Not because they didn't want to talk, gossip was their
mainstay, but because it seemed like hardly anyone
worked every one of their six nights per week, and
anyway, most of them hadn't been at Calendar Girls
longer than six months. The turnover was fast, most of the
girls were doing the work because it could pay well – cash
in hand and no question of needing a green card – and, as
Saz was finding out, it wasn't even too difficult. Most of
them seemed to keep a friendly distance from Mr James,
either because they were scared of him or he was just dis-
interested – Saz had yet to find out. What did seem to be
well known was that he was singularly uninterested in
American women, and that if he ever did date any of the
girls it was always those from "elsewhere" – Europe,
England, Asia – definitely not those just arrived in town
from the West Coast. True, most of the women admitted
that he was attractive, but then most of the women were
also in the work solely for the money and very glad to get
out the door as soon as their shifts ended.

She pocketed her receipt for another sale of champagne
and made two mental notes – one, now that she knew
September might have been faking her appearance, she'd

have to go back and check all the other women she'd elim-
inated because of wrong hair or eye colour – another forty
at least, and two, if September could earn so much doing
this four times a year why had she needed John Clark's
money? The thought of the first September broke her day-
dream and Saz crossed the room to where James was
waiting.

"I just thought I'd check how you're getting on, come in to
my office and we'll have a chat."

Saz followed him into the room. It was pretty much the
blueprint office of any successful businessman – padded
leather couch, polished mahogany table, full drinks
cabinet, a few tasteful prints and very little that actually
looked like it could function in a working office other than
the imposing desk where Mr James now took a seat. The
kind of desk Saz just wished that the over-officious Colleen
from the Enterprise Allowance office could see her sitting
behind. He motioned her to sit down opposite him.

"Well, September, you seem to be doing very well indeed."
    Saz put on her friendly, slightly stupid face.
    "Yeah, thanks Mr James. To tell the truth I'm enjoying
it a lot more than I thought I would."
    "You thought you wouldn't like it?"
    "No, not that, I just didn't know if I'd be any good at it,
but it's quite fun really."
    "Have you given any thought to how long you'll be
staying with us then?"
    "Oh, well, as I told you, I do plan to move on in a week
or so . . ."
    "Once you've got what you came for?"
    Saz was startled out of her dippy persona.
    "Sorry?"

"What you came for – building up the bank balance. Adding to the travel fund?"

Her pulse slowly descended to its usual rate.

"Oh, yes. Building up the bank balance. Right."

James got up and went over to the drinks cabinet.

"English. Now let me see – gin and tonic?"

"Um, oh all right, yes, I'll make an exception this one time – please."

"Never did know an English girl to refuse a gin!" He smarmed and handed her the glass.

"Have you been travelling long?"

"A few months."

"I guess your funds must be pretty low then huh?"

"Well, yes, but this seems to be doing the trick."

"You're very good at the job you know September, you could stay on longer if you wanted. Or come back maybe, in a few months."

"Well, yes, I suppose I could."

She took another gamble, thinking of what Charlie had told her about the other September's work habits.

"I mean, I love New York. It would be wonderful to be able to come back three or four times a year."

"Become one of my regulars, you mean?"

James was smiling now, looking more relaxed.

"Yes, I suppose I do."

Saz smiled back at him, trusting this tall, extremely good-looking man less and less with every sip of her too-strong gin.

"Well, we'll see what we can do, yeah September? Time you got back to work now. I'll see you tomorrow."

"And that's all he said?" Caroline muttered, valiantly trying to stay awake while Saz changed and told her the story of her evening's work.

"That's it. I've got three theories now. Wanna hear them?"

"Do I have any choice? You might as well tell me, you're only going to keep me awake all night trying to work it out in your head if you don't say them out loud."

"OK. Theory Number One – he's running a drugs ring and is going to ask me to take a . . . a CD of Neil Sedaka's 'Calendar Girl' back to London for a friend, but actually it's really a cleverly disguised stash of cocaine."

"Some drugs ring. The amount of coke he'd fit into a CD is hardly going to make him Mr Big of the Underworld!"

"Well, we'll know when the time comes for him to give me my going away present won't we? Stop interrupting. Theory Number Two – he's a member of the mafia . . ."

"With a name like Simon James? Shouldn't he be called Riccardo or Giorgio?"

"Right, he'd really name himself after a perfume! James is just a pseudonym. And the gambling tables are a cleverly disguised way of laundering stolen funds."

"Marginally more possible. But unlikely given just how drunk you've told me the gamblers get. However if it is the case then I think you'd better leave New York now and never come back! You may be my ex-lover, but an ex-lover with a concrete overcoat, I don't need!"

"Don't you mean concrete boots?"

"Not once you've spent the winter in New York you don't. Theory Number Three?"

"I'm not sure, I don't have it clear in my head yet, but I think it's something else. Something to do with the wigs and the pretence and the falsity. I think maybe September enjoyed the game of it."

"Oh please! She'd come all this way just for the fantasy? Hell, she could get that in Streatham for a tube fare."

"Not any more she couldn't. Anyway, I do."

"Do what?"

"Enjoy the role playing. I quite like it. New hair, new name. It's exciting."

"Yeah, but lying's part of what you do for a living."

"Thanks, you put it so nicely. Well, maybe she was a frustrated actress. Maybe that's the only reason she did it."

"Right. That and the money."

"Oh yeah, the money. Well maybe she's just a con-artist. Conning drunks to buy champagne and conning John Clark to give her all his money. Perhaps she's the baddie after all."

"You think so?"

"I don't know. Everything else just seems so extreme. I know Calendar Girls sounds like something out of a movie, but actually all the girls are really nice, and it's not as if we don't know plenty of women in London who've paid their way by hostessing."

"Yeah Saz, only most of them were gay."

"Who's to say September isn't? John Clark said they were 'friends' – he was very clear on that. And I believe him – I don't think he's the type to have an affair . . ."

"What's 'the type'?"

"You are Carrie, remember? Now shut up and listen. So we assume she wasn't shagging Mr Clark and though I don't like James, that's more because he's just one of those slimy arrogant men, than because he might be . . . whatever he might be. But none of the girls would seriously consider having an affair with him – the odd fling maybe, but he certainly isn't take home to your mother material. All the same, I think he is exactly what he seems. . ."

"And what's that?"

"A slightly nasty, definitely shady bloke, who's involved in something which is bigger than just the facade of 'Calendar Girls' – but that's all. It's not as if we haven't come across similar set-ups back home."

"Yeah sweetheart, but neither of us have ever actually worked in them."

"I know, but you know what they're like, you've heard the stories – it's bound to be to do with gambling or drugs or whatever . . . but despite everything, the strangest person here is still September herself right? The woman who comes over here regularly from London, who has dinner with John Clark and who no-one seems to be able to put a name to. So the answer must lie with her. I still need to get closer to her."

"Check his records."

"CDs?"

"No! Records stupid! He must have personnel records. Go through them. See what he's got on her."

"Well how do I do that?"

"Oh for God's sake Saz, you're the 'detective' here, remember? How on earth did you persuade them to give you that Enterprise Allowance?"

"Told them there was a lot of debt collection work in south-east London. Funnily enough, they believed me. What's that got to do with it?"

"Well you'll have to get access to his files somehow – I don't know, break in, scale the drainpipe, bribe the cleaner, marry the owner . . . do some detecting!"

"I hate all that climbing through windows in the middle of the night shit."

"When have you ever done it?"

"I haven't, I just hate the idea."

"Then walk through the door in broad daylight – which I might point out, is only a few hours away and some of us have creative work to do tomorrow – go to sleep."

"OK, sorry. Goodnight."

Saz turned out the light and thought for a while as she watched the lights from the cars in the street play with the shadows on the ceiling.

"Hey Carrie?"

"Yes? What?"

"Do they deal in microfilm at that college of yours?"

"Microfilm?"

"Yeah, you know, like in the movies?"

"Oh Lordy! I'll find out. I suppose you'd need a micro camera too?"

"I guess so. Do you think they do exist in real life, now that the Kremlin's dead?"

"Sweetheart – this is America – the Iron Curtain may be dead but the FBI and the CIA are alive and kicking. I expect we can find you some secondhand spy equipment from somewhere."

"How exciting!"

"Yeah. Just don't get caught! How are you going to get hold of his files anyway?"

"I don't know. I'll dream on it and then work it out when I go for my run tomorrow. Something will come up. Something always comes up."

"Yeah, like daybreak – shut up!"

"OK. Goodnight sidekick."

"See you in the morning gumshoe."

CHAPTER 15

Easter eggs and matzos

Things calmed down after that. She called her parents and told them we were going away – we didn't, but it meant she didn't have to visit them for about a month. She stayed with me, we stayed together. My gym routine lapsed, she came straight home after work. When I didn't have gigs in the evenings we'd spend those dark hours together. I started cancelling work. It was like the first days of our relationship – only soft and calm – wanting to be with each other all the time like at the beginning, but now knowing each other so less frenetic, less panicked – we were in love again. I wanted to spend all day in bed with her, lying beside her smooth skin, cocooned in our relationship.

I didn't know she'd already begun her own metamorphosis.

She'd come home, I'd make dinner and then we'd watch a film or just go straight to bed, lying thigh to thigh, two lots of smooth girls' skin lying alongside each other, we'd hold hands and look up at the ceiling. In the weekends we stayed in bed until three or four, just getting up to eat and drink and then back to our nest. It wasn't so much the draw of sex as the lure of each other. She was magnetic for me. I didn't want to be away from her. She started coming to gigs with me – she didn't like to come in, it was too smoky, too loud, there were too many other people. She'd drop me off and I'd run in, have a quick drink, do the twenty minute set, collect my money and run out again to where she was waiting for me in the car. What used to be an evening's work, a social event talking to the other comics, became a quick hour-long trip so we could run back to our burrow. It was late winter and I felt like we were hibernating. Storing up our love against the long dark nights. I like the dark, it's safe.

I dreaded the spring.

The first weekend in March we went to Brighton. It was still very cold but we went for the tacky couple fun of it. To walk along the pier eating candy floss, to eat fish and chips within smelling distance of the sea, to skim stones on the barely rippling surf. We went to the Pavilion and gloried in its campness. She pictured herself pale and delicate on a chaise longe, I pictured myself roasting lamb on the spit in the kitchen. We both saw ourselves making love in the King's four poster bed, on the cold flagstone floors of the kitchen, hidden behind the curtains of the music room. We both saw ourselves making love – saw it, we didn't do it much that weekend though. We lay together quietly and talked of dreams instead. The Pavilion dragons everywhere came alive and spoke to us of quests and journeys and dreaming and we went back to our B&B and slept, holding hands, legs entwined.

I dreamt I woke up and she was gone. She told me she didn't dream. But I'd heard her cry out in her sleep and I said she must have. She said maybe it wasn't her, maybe I'd heard somebody else crying.

But I know what her tears sound like.

We drove home through little country roads, avoiding the motorway – we went to see the site of the battle of Hastings. I marvelled at how one event can change history, she bought an art deco teapot. We brought home chutney and marmalade and lemon curd and a big bag of potatoes from the stall on the side of the road. We went away for a weekend and brought home more bricks and mortar to build up the wall of our domestic life.

I'd stopped calling Dolores. I didn't really think about it, it just happened. It wasn't intentional, I hadn't wanted her to know when I'd been unhappy and now that things were OK, I didn't want to deal with anyone who might rock the boat. Dolores hadn't been that close for a long time either. Her relationship with Annie was better than any she'd had in a long time and I assumed she didn't miss me. She called me three times and each time I listened to the message on the answerphone and decided not to reply. I listened to a lot of messages at the time. I wasn't interested in having conversations with anyone but the Woman with the Kelly McGillis Body. And I only wanted to have conversations with her soul. And her body. Which was more like talking in braille.

As I do now.

Eyes closed, not looking, not talking, just feeling to converse with her body. And her soul.

I was cutting myself off in order to entrench myself even further in our relationship and words seemed pointless.

Dolores didn't think so. One day I chose to pick up the phone. Bad choice.

"Maggie?"

"Yes."

"Where the hell have you been?"

"Here."

"Didn't you get my messages?"

"Yes."

"And?"

"And nothing."

"What? Are you all right?"

"I'm fine Dolly, I just don't really feel like talking at the moment."

"You haven't felt like talking for months."

"No. I haven't."

"Is it her?"

"Yes it is her. But not in the way that you mean. It is her in that I don't want anyone else. In that I don't know why you're calling."

"What the fuck are you on Maggie? I'm calling because I'm your friend and when I don't hear from you for ages – literally months – I get worried."

"You don't need to."

"Maggie! I heard you were working out like a maniac. Then I heard you were cancelling gigs left, right and centre."

"Both right – your grapevine is flourishing! But there's nothing to worry about. I only want to be with her."

"But I heard . . ."

"I'm sure you did, Dolly. I'm sure you heard all sorts of things. And now you've heard me. I don't want any inter- ference, I don't want any phone calls, I just want to be left alone."

"OK. OK babe, if that's what you want, I won't call again. I'm sorry. I'm your friend Maggie, I just want you to know that."

"I do know it Dolores."

"I hope so."

"I do. Give my love to Annie. Bye."

I hung up. Absurdly pleased with myself at having burnt yet another bridge. Happy to have cut out my oldest friend. I wasn't thinking clearly.

But I am now.

That was March. And then it was Passover again. Cleaning the flat. Clearing it out. Lent and the lead up to Passover. One season of deprivation and cleansing leading into another, both with a finale of feasting and celebration. Thanksgiving and rebirth combined. Like a wake and a christening. Jesus celebrated Passover. But when he rode into Jerusalem on a donkey it was to have the Passover meal with his friends, not his family. He must have disappointed his mother. Thirty three and still unmarried.

She was going "home" for Passover. Like our place was not her home – after four years. I didn't mind so much this time, after all the pain of winter I felt secure. Scoured. Cleansed and safe. So she went "home" for Passover.

April is the cruellest month. Not because of the lilacs. Lilacs unearth themselves. But because I started scrabbling around in what I thought was dead earth and I discovered nettles – very much alive and sharp and stinging.

In the early afternoon of Good Friday, our kitchen clean even of hot cross buns, she left to go to her parents' house. I had a short sleep in front of the television – the story of Barabas not holding the same appeal that it had when I was a child – and then I got up and went into our room.

I had the cleaning bug. Celebrating Jewish festivals with your partner is all very well, but it's easier to do when your partner is with you. When they go "home" to mummy and daddy and you're still trying to obey the rules, it can be a little trying. Four years and I'd never once had so much as a slice of toast during Passover – I'd never developed much of an appetite for matzos either – but I liked the idea of "keeping faith" with her. Only she got to go and eat and drink celebration meals with the family, I was staying at home for a boiled egg by myself. So I had the cleaning bug. It was four in the afternoon – three hours to sundown and just enough time to clean out the bedroom cupboards.

I started with the drawers, throwing out old cotton buds, plastic bags. Junking pairs of holey tights I'd never wear again and happily filling rubbish bags with tired pieces of the recent past. I made piles – things I knew I didn't want, things I might want and things I'd have to ask her if it was OK to throw out. Eventually, at about six, I came to a halt. I bravely threw out both the "definite no" and the "maybe" piles and put the "ask her" pile into a plastic bag for disposal at the back of the cupboard above the wardrobe. Standing on a chair, I pulled down the fifteen or so winter jumpers we share so I could put the "maybe" bag behind them. There was a small suitcase there. I pulled it down to make room and as I did so the single clasp flew open and the contents of the case fell on top of me. I got off the chair to pick the stuff up and put it back. It wasn't much, a couple of thin little cocktail type dresses that I hadn't seen her wear for a long time, a flimsy pair of shoes and an envelope.

I know I shouldn't have opened it. I ruined Christmas for myself once, I was about seven, both my parents were at

work and I opened all my presents – saw what they were
and then re-wrapped them very carefully so no-one would
know I'd done it. Christmas morning came and not a yule-
tide surprise in sight. But I pretended. How I pretended –
couldn't risk mummy and daddy finding out. Pretended all
day and went to bed with a sick feeling in the bottom of
my stomach. You'd think I'd have learnt my lesson. It
wasn't addressed to me. It wasn't addressed to anyone.
But I couldn't help myself. I think I've said before, I
always want to know everything. Curiosity kills and all
that, unfortunately I don't have a cat's nine lives. Or its
indifference.

The envelope wasn't sealed, it was folded into itself.
Inside was a card. It was dated the day of my birthday.

> Thanks for another lovely evening,
> hope you had a great time in New York,
> all my love, John.

And it was signed with kisses.

I dropped the card and ran in to the bathroom to throw
up. She'd lied to me. Lies on top of lies. I threw up until I
had nothing more inside me. I lay with my head against
the cool white of the toilet bowl. Lay for an hour or more,
my world reeling. Then I got up, left her stuff where it
was, packed a bag and walked out. I didn't know where I
was going or for how long, but I had no intention of
waiting patiently for her to come home. I took all the
spare money either of us had lying around, my keys and
left.

It was early evening when I walked outside. I sat on a bus
for about an hour, got off, got on to the tube and sat on a

train for another hour or so. Then I went to Annie's house where Dolores took one look at me, gave me a fiercely strong gin and tonic and put me to bed.

I hoped never to wake up again. I dreamt of lilacs.

But you always do wake up into the nightmare don't you?

CHAPTER 16

Tightrope walking

Saz waited until most of the customers had left. It was 3am, she walked out on to the balcony at the back of the building and collected her thoughts. In another hour the whole place would be hers, she could get the information she needed and leave New York the next day. She breathed in a cold blast of air from the night and walked back into the lounge.

"What are you doing hiding out there, September?"

Saz was startled to find Simon James a few feet behind her. He hadn't been in all night and it was unusual for him to turn up so late. In the five minutes she'd been out on the balcony, the room had cleared of the last clients and they were alone.

"Oh, Mr James, you startled me."

"Why September, what have you got to hide?"

"Nothing, it's just that I thought there wasn't anyone here, and well . . . this is New York after all."

"Yes, of course, New York, how silly of me to forget. The city of sin and muggers and a murder every three minutes – that's what you English think isn't it?"

"Something like that Mr James."

James moved across to Saz and sat on the chair beside her.

"Well, perhaps we're not quite as bad as the movies paint us. I'd like you to call me Simon, September. Would you join me for a drink?"

"Ah, well . . . Simon, I really should be getting back, it's very late."

"One little drink?"

Now that he was closer, Saz could see that James was actually very drunk, the thin lines of red veins standing out on his fine chiselled cheekbones and the tart smell of whisky on his breath. He reached out and took her hand.

"I really do like English girls, you know September."

Saz decided to play along, reasoning that James couldn't be any more forceful or arrogant than the men she'd been dealing with nightly for the past week.

"And I like American men, Simon. Let me fix you that drink."

Saz crossed to the bar, where she mixed herself a gin and tonic, containing about as much gin as one ripe juniper berry and a very large whisky for James.

"Ice?"

"Yes please."

He slurred a smile across at her and Saz added the ice to his whisky.

"Here's hoping you crash on the rocks any minute now," she thought.

Saz sat with Simon James for the next hour, in which time he had three more large whiskys and told her most of his life story – poor kid, violent father, loving mother, too many in the family, older sister died in a nasty car accident, brother stayed in small town, worked hard, achieved nothing, whereas he worked hard, made a few "wise investments" and was now "comfortably off". Saz, looking at his Rolex and Cartier cufflinks couldn't help comparing his idea of comfortably off to her dream of a new answerphone. She also knew that she believed his story about "wise investments" almost as much as she believed the one he was starting to tell her now about how his wife didn't understand him.

Steering him away from the subject of his unsatisfactory home life, Saz went back to the question of the business.

"But tell me about how you set yourself up here. I mean, it's a . . . well, it's a great place . . . and if, as you said, you had such a difficult childhood, then it's all the more impressive that you're doing so well now."

By this time, Saz had manoeuvred herself so that she was sitting on the floor at his feet, looking as close as she could manage like the doting acolyte and Simon James, like so many good-looking men before him, couldn't believe that Saz wasn't really solely interested in his glorious tales of derring-do.

Simon James smiled the expansive smile of a rich, drunk man and began.

"Well, honey – what I did was I made sure to listen."

Saz nodded.

"Always listen and never interrupt – and I learnt things. I worked evenings and weekends while I was in high school, saved every cent and then I travelled – I went to casinos all over Europe and the States and met men – wealthy men, businessmen, and other men so rich they had no interest in business, and I'd drink with them and listen to them and they'd tell me what they wanted. It was kind of like taking a survey."

"But how did you get the money to go to all the clubs?"

"Didn't I just tell you not to interrupt honey?"

"Sorry, I'm just interested – interested in you, I mean."

Saz smiled and James started again.

"I didn't say I wasn't working, I was doing odd jobs – delivering and stuff like that – nothing too messy though, I like to keep my hands clean. I won't have dirty fingernails. And I listened, I heard what those men had to say. I decided to set up the sort of club they wanted – supply and demand, give the public what they want."

"And here it is?"

"Yeah, here it is. Plenty of blondes, dark eyes, clever girls who know how to talk and when to keep their mouths shut and no whores. No sluts. I can't tell you how important that is – these men can get any woman they want – they don't have to pay for it and they don't want to be mixing with the sort of women that sell."

Saz smiled, hating him all the more and forbore to mention that in her opinion changing your hair and eye colour and flattering leery old men was just as much a form of prostitution as the traditional method, merely adding, "Yes, but we do take money off them though, don't we?"

"Yeah, and they know that. They don't mind paying exorbitant amounts for good champagne, that's part of the game they're prepared to play, but they aren't prepared to pay for women. Any women."

"No," thought Saz, "And that's what makes them the cheap bastards they are."

"You know," he continued, downing his whisky and holding out an unsteady glass for Saz to refill, "What they like best about this place, is that it's safe – my God! The deals that go on here! Mostly up there in July," he said referring to the bridge room at the top of the house, "They partner up and use the pairing for business deals, I've watched it happen, it's kind of like a blind date – if they find someone they can play well with, then they can expect to do good business with them. There's more partnerships made here than on the Love Boat, honey."

James was starting to slow down now, and Saz still wanted more. While providing a place for business men to do deals was probably shady, depending on what they were dealing in, it was hardly illegal and Saz had a feeling that James still knew a lot more than even he, in his arrogance, was prepared to say. She put on a look of complete little girl innocence and asked, "And the English girls, Simon? What do they think of us?"

"Christ! Girls! You're so bloody self-centred!" James laughed at her, "Here I am, telling you about some of the greatest business minds in the latter part of the twentieth century, and all you want to know is 'Am I pretty enough?' Oh God! Women! I'll tell you what they think about you English girls – they think you make perfect pigeon pie!"

James roared at his joke and pulled Saz up on to her knees so she was kneeling directly in front of him, he held her right arm tight while he ruffled her hair with his free hand.

"They think, September – and let me tell you, ALL English girls are called September, it's because that was the first time I was ever there . . . They call themselves what they want, but I call them September. And my businessmen think that with your expertise with tea trays and plates of scones that you're the finest carriers anywhere in the world."

Saz, wondering just how dumb she could get away with, said "Oh?"

"Don't play stupid with me babe, you know what I mean, you're a smart girl, you must be, or I wouldn't have taken you on."

"Stupid?"

"Yeah, are you telling me you don't know what a pigeon is honey?"

"No. OK. But I am telling you I've never been one."

"Don't worry darling, everyone has to start somewhere. Now take my jacket and we'll see where you can start."

Saz took James' jacket and feeling in the pocket the unmistakable weight of a handgun she placed it as far as possible from him on a chair by the door. While she was there she dimmed the lights even lower and fixed him yet another whisky. She crossed to where he was sprawled in the big leather armchair, handed him the drink and asked if he would like a foot rub.

"Yes darling, I'd love that – you start there. Hah! At my feet – that's a good place to start."

James lay back, took a long draught of the whisky and closed his eyes. Saz slipped his shoes off, mentally blessed her reflexology teacher and began to send Simon James off into one of the soundest sleeps of his life.

When he'd been snoring for over fifteen minutes, Saz got up and left the room, making immediately for his office downstairs.

It was four thirty by now and the building was empty. Street lights were the only illumination, that and the dim light from the room where James slept. She left the door open slightly and hurried down the two flights of stairs to James' office, stopping at the girls' changing room to pick up her bag and coat. It was as she'd expected, James' elaborate security arrangements, of which he was justifiably proud, were not yet in operation, needing his personal key to turn the system on. And his office door was still unlocked – James had an old fashioned dressing room with bed adjacent to his office and had evidently been expecting to get her down there before he fell asleep.

She walked in and turned on the desk light. A blotter with a few non-specific doodles and two silver framed photos – one that was probably his wife – brunette interestingly enough and one of an old woman, a black and white photo of a woman peering uncertainly into the camera. "So you didn't lie about your beloved Mama then Simon! Good boy. I'm sure she'd be very proud of you now!"

She tried the drawers. The top one was unlocked and contained a few messages, nothing of much interest – except the keys to the other drawers.

"God! You're more trusting than I would be."

She tried the drawers, the second contained a mirror, a few blades and a small crystal box of what tasted to Saz like almost pure Columbian.

"Now we're getting somewhere. Shame I'm a fitness freak these days!"

The next drawer down had a lot of files – mostly on tax and wages.

"Well, James, if I wanted to get you, I'm sure I could just send this on to the IRS, but unfortunately I've got prettier fish to fry."

She locked both drawers, replaced the keys in the top one and turned to the filing cabinet. This was easier, for while Saz knew it would be locked, she also knew exactly how to open it with a small paper clip from the desk. She began to go systematically through the files. Nothing in the top drawer, it was all building deeds, land rates and other papers which, while bound to be suspect, were not of much relevance to the original September.

In the third drawer Saz found what she'd come for. A file which, month by month, day by day, listed all the girls.

"What Colleen of the good ship Enterprise Allowance wouldn't give for me to keep records like this!"

Saz lifted out the "September" file and reeled when she saw that the first few pages neatly clipped together were her own. She felt a heavy feeling in the pit of her stomach as she read the comments in James' unmistakable sprawling handwriting:

NAME : 'Mary' (pseudonym?)
CONTACT : Janice Green ('June' 1987/88). NB
– call asap.
HAIR : peroxide

EYES : natural (dark brown)
STATUS: untried (intends return UK some
weeks, suggests more visits US) – regular??

On the back of the page was Caroline's telephone number with a note to check her address.

There were four more Septembers in the file, some with not yet peroxided hair, and Saz decided to photograph rather than steal them. She reached into her bag and pulled out the tiny camera Caroline had managed to get for her and, praying that it would work correctly, she began to photograph the other sheets of paper – the others all had extra pages which Saz didn't bother to read, if they were to do with whatever "pigeoning" James had been talking about, she'd need to check up on flights and dates anyway and now was certainly not the time to start analyzing the data.

She was just taking the last photo when she heard James' steps on the stairs above her. He shouted out, "September? Are you still here?"

Saz shoved the "September" file back, closed the cabinet as quietly as she could, relocked it and threw the camera in her bag. Grabbing her bag and coat she ran into the dressing-room, closing the door behind her.

Simon James crashed into his office and immediately checked the drawers of both his desk and his filing cabinet. He then kicked open the door of his dressing-room, switching on the bright overhead light and pointing the gun right at Saz's head, he demanded:

"What the fuck are you doing in here?"

CHAPTER 17

Bodily functions

Saz looked up from where she lay naked on the bed, covered only by a sheet, smiled and said, "Waiting for you, Simon. What else?"

James laughed. After years in the business this was what he'd come to expect from a lot of the girls who worked for him. He'd had an idea that maybe this one was different though. A feeling at the back of his mind that there was something else she was after. But no, in the end this girl was like all the others – peroxide blonde or natural, they were, after all, women. He put the gun down and loosened his tie.

"I didn't mean to fall asleep back there honey, hope I didn't keep you waiting for too long."

"Oh no, Simon," Saz purred. "That's fine, it gave me a chance to come down here and get comfortable. Nice bed! It's very . . . spacious. And this photo, is it your mother?"

Saz pointed to the photo on his bedside table – it was unmistakably the same woman as the one framed on his desk, only in this photo the woman was years younger and smiling directly at the camera, the ocean behind her and small waves around her ankles.

"Yeah. We were on vacation. Maine. My father wasn't with us – it was a great holiday. Hot. Sunny. And completely irrelevant. Come over here, September."

Simon was slurring his words slightly, but not enough for Saz to assume he was still very drunk, unfortunately his little nap seemed to have re-energised him. She quickly weighed up her options and decided that playing along for the moment was her best chance. So, letting the sheet drop away from her, she slid out of the bed and walked across to James. He studied her body as she crossed the room.

"You've got a fine physique babe. Do you work out?"

"Not much Simon. I run. Swim a little. I don't like the idea of a gym. I don't like to get all hot and sweaty in front of too many people. I prefer to get sweaty with just one other person around, if you know what I mean."

Simon James did. He grabbed her left arm and pulled her to him. The swiftness of his movement and the cold silk of his shirt against her skin surprised her and Saz let out a gasp of breath. Simon James took this for a gasp of pleasure. He started to kiss her. Now Saz knew she was definitely in trouble. Either she could go along with it, have sex with a man for the first time in almost eight years, though at least on the last occasion she'd actually wanted to do so, or – and this was the much more appealing choice – find a way to get out of it. However, given that she'd decided to climb in James' bed because it seemed safer than having him find her up to her armpits in the filing cabinet, it would look a bit strange for her to back out now. She supposed it was unlikely that James would have enough of an idea of modern feminism to grasp the politically correct concept of "I changed my mind and I have every right to do so". In fact she had more than a sneaking suspicion that he'd be turned on by bullying her into having sex with him. Or worse. Her escape route would have to be much more careful than that. And as he ran his finely manicured nails down her back and held her against his smooth, stubble-free cheek, she realised she'd need a better excuse than any of the ones that were running through her head. James pulled her closer, his fine wool suit rubbing against her skin. She started to kiss him back, all the time her brain racing for an excuse, any reason to back out. James pushed her down on to the bed. Saz rolled around and began to massage his back.

"Let me help you relax, Simon."

James turned and tried to kiss her again.

"I don't want to relax, sweetheart. Calming down is the last thing on my mind."

He wasn't lying. Saz slipped out from under him, and preparing to accept the inevitable began to excuse herself.

"I'm going to have to go to the bathroom, Simon."

"What is it, what's wrong?"

"Nothing, nothing at all, you're a great guy Simon – but I don't want to have your baby."

James smiled and lay back.

"Right. I think you'll find everything you need in the cabinet on the left. Don't be long though, I don't want to cool down."

Saz smiled and ran her hand down his long, taut thigh as she left the room.

"No, I won't be long."

Saz sauntered into the bathroom, sashaying across the room in her best imitation of a naked Mae West.

About half an hour later she dressed as quickly as she could, picked up her bag and coat from the chair and walked to the door.

"I'll see you tomorrow Simon. Goodnight."

"Yeah."

"And that was it. I ran most of the way home, leaving him there to sulk like a little boy!"

Caroline and Saz lay laughing on the bed as the thin morning sunlight filtered through the blinds.

"I can't believe you got away with it!"

"Well, he was pretty pissed, maybe he was just looking for an excuse to go to sleep!"

"But you actually cut yourself?"

"Yeah. Extreme I know, but I'd rather have a small nick on my toe than . . . well, than fuck him."

Saz had taken a gamble on the fact that she knew American men to be usually more fastidious than their English counterparts, how they generally had a disgust of body hair on women and that disgust was likely to extend to the normal bodily functions of womankind as well. She also knew that James was particularly fussy about everything being spotlessly clean, he went crazy if any of the girls had so much as a speck of dirt on their clean white shirts, so she couldn't imagine him allowing her to soil his smooth silk sheets. She'd gone to the bathroom, taken out his old-fashioned safety razor and made a tiny nick on the underside of her big toe. And then, with a few drops of blood on her upper thigh, she'd walked back into the room. She dived for her bag, pulling out a couple of tampons and chattered on a little more, looked up at where he lay on the bed. He was fully dressed and armed, she was naked and vulnerable, and yet she knew she'd won as the erection he'd been so forcefully pushing against her, quickly subsided.

"Shit!"

"I'm sorry Simon, really I am. I'll make it up to you."

Saz reached out to stroke his arm and when he flinched at her touch, she knew she could push it even further.

"I mean, if you'd like me to do anything else . . .?"

"No! It's fine. Just go home and let me get some sleep. I've wasted most of the damn night on you, now piss off!"

"I'm sorry. Really I am Simon."

Saz sunk her teeth into another doughnut and burst out laughing again.

"God Carrie, you should have seen his face!"

She'd picked up coffee and doughnuts on her way back to Caroline's because she knew she had to wake her and tell the story of the great escape and she also knew that Caroline would only be happy to hear the tale if she came bearing gifts of food as well.

"Christ Saz, you're lucky!"

"Luck had nothing to do with it kiddo, sheer brilliance in the face of almost impossible odds is how I like to look at it!"

"Yeah, but don't you think it's a bit politically suspect to plead 'period'?"

"I didn't 'plead' it. He assumed. You think I should have done it?"

"No. But you could have used the opportunity to educate him in the joys of the natural workings of the female body!"

"Right Carrie. Well, you're welcome to take him a copy of *Our Bodies, Ourselves* if you want, I'd just as soon leave him ignorant if you don't mind."

"OK, so what now?"

"Now I get the first flight home and you print up these photos as soon as you can so that I can study the information while I'm on the plane."

"What did you manage to take?"

"I got one of each of the September files."

"Good move, but doesn't he still have my phone number?"

"Yeah. I'll call the phone company and get them to give you a new one. That's the only thing of yours I gave him. I said I couldn't remember the address – he was supposed to get it from me tomorrow, but I guess he'll have to wait. I'll leave you the cash to pay for changing the number, I certainly earned enough in the past week! So, how soon can you get the photos developed?"

"This afternoon I suppose. I'll go into college and do them first thing. Why don't you call the airports and find out what time you'll be able to get a plane?"

Saz went to call while Caroline got dressed. She was just finishing the last doughnut when Saz came back.

"I called the phone company and that's OK, you'll have a new number by the day after tomorrow – money's on the hall table. And there's a flight from JFK to Heathrow at six thirty this evening. So if you think you can get the photos done by then, I'll book a seat."

"Just. They won't be ready by the time you have to leave here, you'll need to go early to pay for the ticket. I'll come out to the airport with them, I should make it by about four."

"Good. Just one other thing and I'll start packing."

"What's that?"

"To make double sure that you get no hassle from Simon James, I'm going to leave him a 'Dear John' letter. Tell him I'm off travelling again or something."

"Thanks. I mean, I do want to get to know some New Yorkers but he's not exactly top of my list of locals to get friendly with."

Saz put the envelope in a postbox at the airport. It was carefully worded and just crass enough to sound believable.

Dear Simon,
First of all let me apologize for not seeing you
in person, but I honestly couldn't bear to say
goodbye. I'm so sorry last night ended the way
it did. It was certainly something I'd been

hoping for and I hope you had too. But I guess
it just wasn't meant to be. I haven't been
entirely honest with you Simon. To tell the
truth I do have a boyfriend, but I let my
attraction to you blind me to my
responsibilities to him. Our relationship hasn't
been good for some time now and I guess I was
just using you to see how I felt about him. Well,
the truth is, that I've discovered I love him.
There. I've said it. And I guess I owe that
knowledge to you. I'm going back to him now to
try to get things right. Thank you.
With love,
            September.

She'd wondered about the "with love" but decided he was
probably arrogant enough to accept it at face value and it
was certainly common for girls to leave without giving
any notice at all.

The Tannoy was just announcing the last boarding call for
her flight to London when Caroline ran in. Saz grabbed the
file Carrie held out to her.

"Is this them? What took you so long?"

"I had to wait ages to get into the darkroom."

"Thanks hon, you've been brilliant. Tell your dad that
at least the photography course was worth his hard earned
cash! Well sweetheart, it's been great, but I've got to get
. . ."

"Wait!"

"I can't Carrie, I'm late already. Call me if you just have
to tell me you now know you loved me all along."

"No, Saz. Wait! One of the photos."

"Didn't it come out?"

"Yes but . . ."

"Well, what's the problem then? Quick, I'm late."

"I know her!"

"You know who?"

"The girl in the photo – I mean not personally."

"Well what's her name? Do you think she's September?"

"Hold on."

"I can't. The bloody plane's about to go. What's her name for God's sake?"

"I don't know her name. I only ever met her once for about five minutes. She knows Annie."

"Annie Cox?"

"Yeah. She goes out with Maggie. You know, Annie's friend Maggie. Maggie what's-her-name. The stand-up."

"Stand-up? You mean Maggie Simpson?"

"That's it. She's Maggie's girlfriend. Your Simon James has got a photo of Maggie's girlfriend."

CHAPTER 18

Team sports

Saz flew into Heathrow in the early morning and put the precious photos in her bag. She'd spent the past five hours staring at the one of September. Or at least the only September Caroline had recognised. She'd read the file notes – probably as fake as her own and then stared at the photo trying to get the answers from that. The photo was black and white so while she could see the short dark hair, the eye colour was less certain, that they were dark was obvious, but they could also have been hazel or even dark green. And anyway, just because Carrie recognised her didn't mean that she was also John Clark's September. She changed her money, damning "them" for charging so much commission and then made her way home by bus. Her flat, when she finally got home was freezing so, fully dressed and ignoring the insistent light of her answer-phone, she climbed into bed and went to sleep, a last glance at all four Septembers arrayed against her dressing-table mirror.

In the late morning when she woke, her first thought went to them. "OK girls, today's the day! We're going to have lunch with Mr John Clark."

She listened to her messages – three from her mother demanding to know where she was, one from Cassie wanting her to babysit again and one from Helen telling her that John Clark was as clean as a whistle from her point of view.

"He's exactly who he says he is Saz. One wife, two kids and no job." Her faith in John Clark's law abiding nature confirmed, she called him at his home number, hoping that Mrs Clark wouldn't get to the phone first.

"John Clark speaking."

"John, it's Saz Martin."

"Oh . . . er . . . ah . . ."

"Don't worry, is your wife there? Just answer yes or no."

"Yes."

"OK, I'll ask the questions. Any news from your end?"

"No. No news at all."

"Right, well I've got a couple of photos I want you to have a look at. When can we meet?"

"Today? I could meet you for lunch."

"Where we met before? How about two o'clock?"

"Yes, that would be fine. I'll see you then."

Saz put the phone down wondering just what lie he'd use for his wife and then with a heavy sigh called her mother.

John Clark walked into the cafe looking even more tired than when Saz had last seen him. At first he didn't recognise her because of the hair. And when he did he was more than a little taken aback – Saz realised she should have warned him that she'd be sitting there with the same blonde locks as his very own September. After they'd ordered coffee he sat down beside her. He was obviously worried.

"It's the money you see Ms Martin, I'm going to need it soon, I never expected the loan to be out this long. She said she'd only need the money for a couple of weeks – she expected to sort everything out."

"Have you told your wife?"`

"No, I don't want to worry her."

"I would have thought just looking at you would worry her enough. Anyway, you don't have to think about paying me for the time being."

"But what about your flight to New York?"

"I made a little while I was there. Let me explain."

Saz told him about Calendar Girls, especially the part about the brown-eyed blondes but leaving out the more sordid details and presented him with the photos. He looked at all four of them quite closely and seemed about to dismiss the two with dark hair until, with a sharp intake of breath, he grabbed one of them and looked at it very closely.

"This is it. This is her."

"You're sure?"

"Yes, see that scar?"

"Where?"

"A tiny scar just there, under her left eye."

"I can't see anything."

"It is her. It's there all right. That faint line just under her eye. I mean, I know she's got dark hair in this photo – but it's her. It's a dog bite. The scar. She got it years ago. We used to joke about it. She loves dogs you see. And this time her dog was sleeping – she was only young – and she went up and cuddled it and it reared up and bit her. Right across the face. She was lucky not to lose an eye."

"And you used to joke about it?"

"Let sleeping dogs lie. After she'd told me about the dog, that's what she always used to say if I ever asked her anything she didn't want to tell me."

"Why didn't you tell me about the scar before?"

"Well, as you said yourself, you couldn't really see it. Only once you knew it was there, and even then you'd have to look for it. I didn't think it would help."

"I asked you to tell me everything."

"I'm sorry. But it doesn't matter now, does it? Not now that you've found her? Did you meet her? Is she living in New York? Did you speak to her about me?"

"Hold on. No, I didn't meet her. I actually think she's here in London. As it turns out, she may be the friend of a friend of a friend. I'm not sure yet, but if she is, then we should have this little mess cleared up within the week."

John Clark looked visibly relieved.

"But I wouldn't count on getting your money back John. Strikes me, that a girl who does secret part-time work as a very well-paid hostess might have some quite good reasons for getting rid of sixteen thousand pounds pretty damn fast."

"No, Ms Martin. It'll be OK. Once I see her. Just give me a chance to talk to her."

"I'll do my best."

Saz left the cafe wondering about the sort of man who could be so besotted as to believe the stories of this "September". She decided that despite his grey exterior, John Clark must be possibly the most romantic man she knew. Or just plain stupid.

That evening she rang Judith and Helen and Claire to invite them all for dinner the next night. Leaving messages on both phones she gave them little choice but to be there.

"And like the loyal friends you are, you will cancel all previous engagements in order to eat my delicious food and hear about how I narrowly escaped death while breaking and entering in New York."

All three women turned up promptly at 8pm.

Over the guacamole Saz filled them in on the basic details up until she went to New York. As she filled the taco shells she told them about Caroline. As she opened the third bottle of wine she told them about Calendar Girls. And how it feels to have a gun pointing at your head.

Claire declared her completely mad and Helen and Judith put on WPC faces as they tut-tutted, but all three greedily grabbed the photo of "September" when Saz produced it. Unfortunately none of them knew Dolores and only Claire had seen Maggie Simpson performing "funnily enough, without her girlfriend", so none of them could confirm Carrie's belief. September's true identity still unknown, they went back to discussing the events in New York.

"And you believe it was good coke?"

"Yes Jude. I do."

"And you'd really know?"

"Well, I'd have a better idea than you! Remember the party we all went to in that really flash warehouse, a couple of years ago?"

"In Camden?"

"Yeah."

"I don't remember it, are you sure I was there?"

"Yes Claire, you were there and the reason you probably don't remember it is because someone there had some similarly "good" cocaine. I remember Helen and Jude both discreetly left the room."

"So we didn't have to face the old 'Oh no! My friends are taking drugs!' dilemma."

"And left me to fry my brains. Right, I do remember now. Thanks a lot girls!"

"But as I was saying, that was the best I'd ever had. The guy that had it couldn't stop bragging about it. A soap star or something like that I think. Anyway, I gave the stuff in Simon James' desk the barest whisk around my gums, because of course, now that I'm a fitness bunny, I don't do anything as airhead as that – and believe me this was just as good, if not better. And there had to be eight or nine ounces, just sitting there, in an unlocked desk drawer."

"No wonder you didn't put him to sleep for long."

"So, what do we do now?"

"Open another bottle of wine and get detecting girl. Only a bit more carefully this time – I don't fancy defending you in an American court when you get extradited for burglary."

Saz opened the wine and the four women formed a plan of action.

"I'll check out Mr James – I'm sure it's not his real name but I'll run it through and see what we can come up with."

"He might be James Simon, darling."

"Yeah, Jude, and he might be Andrew Lloyd Webber, we can but try."

"Now girls," Claire butted in, seeing that the excess of alcohol was promoting a little inter-relationship rivalry, "I'll call my friend who works in New York. She works for the city government and might have some access to building or ownership papers or whatever they have there. It'll probably cost you though. America's supposed to be the land of perfect civil liberties – unless of course you can afford to buy the opposite."

"Or if you're too poor to buy those liberties in the first place. Don't worry, I can afford it, I made a lot of money in the Big Apple remember?"

"Yeah and nearly got your pips blown out in exchange."

"Thanks Helen, I needed reminding."

"Thought you might. And I'll see what I can find out

about our missing girl. I'll take a copy of her photo and check it against those in our missing persons."

"Great. In that case I'll go to sleep for a couple of weeks while you all do my work for me!"

"Oh no you don't. You're going to a few cabaret places to see Ms Simpson performing and then you're going to find a good excuse to visit this Annie and Dolores. Sounds like you've got a lot in common."

After Helen and Judith had gone, bickering as usual, Saz put Claire to sleep on her sofa-bed. Not so much putting to sleep really, more like lifting a sleeping person from a chair and lying them down. She then went to bed herself, having set her alarm for 6am.

"Four hours sleep Saz Martin, a good run and then a nap. After that you'd better look out Blondie, because I'm gaining ground!"

CHAPTER 19

In the gingerbread house

I stayed with Dolores and Annie – and all the family – for nearly six months. At first she called every day. Two or three times a day. I'd hear the phone and crawl under the covers of the bed. Hide in the dark.

It's safer in the dark. I always keep the curtains drawn now.

I stayed in bed for a week and by then the calls had dwindled to one a day. At the same time, seven o'clock every night the phone would ring and I would attempt to stifle the sound with pillows and blankets. Annie always answered the phone and every time she gave the same reply.

"I'm sorry. Maggie doesn't want to speak to you. She can't come to the phone. She's sleeping."

My friends and my misery were combining to make me narcoleptic.

I stay awake now as long as I can. I'm keeping a vigil.

For the first time in my life I discovered the "I can't eat" syndrome. Food made me feel sick, the smell of cooking made me retch, the thought of eating made a dry lump rise in my throat. My body was going through withdrawal. It lasted for about five days and then Keith made me porridge. Porridge is like mashed potato – comfort foods, soft and warm and bland and easy to swallow. Hot, sweet, sticky porridge, made with milk and smothered in brown sugar and cream. Actually, it was too rich and made me throw up, but at least the vomit got me out of bed.

Eventually I got up. I had to. The sheets needed changing and I hated the pictures in the spare room. I cleaned my teeth and discovered I'd lost ten pounds – even grief has its own tarnished silver lining. I went downstairs on the unsteady legs that invalids always descend staircases with – just to make it easier for Mrs Danvers to push them down. Only this time there was no Max to scream at me, just Keith and a fresh pot of coffee. He poured me a cup, passed me the paper and some toast and then went out into the garden.

"There's sunshine out here. It's not such a bad thing."

But it is, sunshine gets into the corners and lets you see the dust motes. I keep the curtains closed and the lights off.

After the coffee I followed him out. I left the toast and *The Independent* on the table, I still had little interest in food and even less in the affairs of the world, mine were more than enough to handle. Besides that, the affairs of the world turn quite slowly, and my life had been turned around in less than two minutes – it takes the earth at least twenty-four hours to do that. Keith was right, not only was there sunshine, but there was also a gentle breeze and birdsong and the sound of children playing in the school yard at the back of the house. It was too much for me and I burst into tears. Keith handed me his huge hanky.

"It's not quite as healthy as tissues, but it always looks good in the movies. I'd light your cigarette for you, only you don't smoke. Do you want to talk about it?"

I snuffled a little into his handkerchief, then a little more into his shoulder and told him what I knew, which obviously wasn't that much, but enough to convince him that my hypothesis was right – she was having an affair. He maintained a respectable pause and then started saying those sensible things that people always feel obliged to say, when really the only thing to do is to say nothing, but they can't bear the silence in case you see it as an opportunity to start crying again:

"Maybe it was only a fling."

"There is a chance they only had dinner."

"Perhaps you should talk to her about it?"

And finally the banality to end all banalities –

"Well, they do say that time heals all wounds."

"I know that Keith, I'm the one that told you that, I've been half an orphan for years now, remember?"

"Only trying to help, and anyway you know it's true."

"I don't care if it's true or not. I don't want it to be true. I don't want to heal. I want to fester. I want it to grow and spread until it bloody well kills her too."

"Hey! Brilliant! She's up and expressing her anger!"

Dolores and Annie strode into the garden from the back door, Dolores carrying shopping bags and grinning her approval of my return to the world and Annie tactfully extricating herself from Dolores' grasp, presumably so as not to remind me of my recent "loss".

My recent loss. It sounds like an obituary.

We all had dinner together that night. The three kids, Dolores and Annie, Keith and I. Just like any other happy, extended family. I almost believed it too, until we were settling down to a good old-fashioned argument about who should do the dishes when the telephone rang. I froze. Nailed stiff to my seat as Dolores and Annie nearly killed each other in a mad dash to get to the phone before I did. Which was a little pointless really, as I couldn't have talked to her even if I'd wanted to, my throat was so dry. Keith and the kids started talking across the table as loudly as possible so I wouldn't have to hear Annie's mumbled

"I'm sorry, I told you, she doesn't want to talk to you."

But I did hear it, my x-ray ears even heard her say my name. Or maybe they didn't, but the shiver that ran down my spine and the convulsions in the pit of my stomach certainly signalled that she had.

I think I hear her whispering for me now, but I know she's not. She can't be.

Annie walked back into the kitchen and took my hand.
    "You know, you can talk to her if you want to."
    "No she bloody well can't, what good will that do?"
    Dolores grabbed my other hand to stake her claim.
    "That bitch has treated her like shit and Maggie doesn't ever have to talk to her again."
    "I'm not saying she does, Doll. I just think, that as Maggie left in such a hurry, there may come a point when she wants to speak to her, and if there does, then that's OK. OK?"
    Annie's voice was calm, but the look she gave Dolores above my head was pure threat and Dolores had no choice but to give in. I was still shaking, so she took me upstairs and tucked me into bed like a small child.

There's nothing like a loss to make you into a child again.
    I feel very small just now.

Still, my new life quickly became routine. I fell into living with all those people like it was the easiest thing in the world. Perhaps it was, certainly living with six other friends has got to be easier than living with one lover in a rotting relationship. Perhaps because it seemed so ordinary, so much like what had been planned for me in my genetic and sociological background. I'd get up with everyone else at about seven thirty in the morning, see them all off to work and school with a smile, and then, to "pay for my keep" I'd do that housework thing – dishes, dust, and vacuum followed by "Woman's Hour" at 10.30am. I'd have my cup of coffee and toast and pretend to be "real". It was like being Snow White. And when the serial was over I'd realise the pretending was over too and I'd climb back into my bed and start to cry again. God knows what the neighbours thought, perhaps they were all at work, perhaps they never heard me. Or maybe they just thought it made perfect sense, all that screaming coming from that "lesbian's house on the corner". I kept it up for nearly three weeks, staying in bed until everyone came home in the evening. I'd get up then for a couple of hours, but I was always asleep by ten o'clock – all that crying wore me out. I almost lost my voice and my eyes stayed red from too many tears and too much sleep.

Perhaps the crying wore her out too.

She stopped calling after the second week. Dolores said Victoria Cook seemed to think she'd gone away. To the States she thought. It seemed to make Dolores angrier than it made me.

"How dare she just piss off and go and have a holiday? Who the hell does she think she is?"

If there is a choice of emotions, Dolly will always take anger – it's over quickest. What pissed me off wasn't the idea of a holiday, but the fact that the information came from Victoria Cook.

I tried to explain how she'd always loved the idea of a trip to America, especially New York. She used to talk about it a lot. Said it was her favourite city. I told her she'd change her mind if she ever actually went there. But she said no, she was sure it would be just as exciting in real life.

I guess she knew what she was talking about after all.

New York certainly can be pretty damn exciting, though she doesn't seem quite so full of its praises now.

CHAPTER 20

Hospital food

Towards the end of my sixth month in Annie's home I began to feel real again. My life had totally changed. I wasn't performing any more, I had none of my own clothes – I'd refused to let Dolores go back to our place and pick things up for me. I hadn't seen any of "our" friends, just those of Dolores, Annie, Keith. All my things, all my books, even my address book was back at our flat. I was starting to feel like a real person again, but I wasn't sure who that person was anymore. I was starting to be a "one" instead of a couple and it was hard to work out exactly what I thought about anything. It was like I'd slowly come alive and on looking around discovered that I'd made my home in limbo.

It had been one of my usual mornings – they were all out, the housework was done and my hour with the radio was just beginning, something about women in management I think and then the phone rang. I was feeling so calm I decided to answer it but even as I picked up the receiver I knew it would be her.

"Maggie?"

Her voice, her soft, sweet voice cut through my calm like a roasting knife cuts through the hot flesh of a chicken, my anger and pain spurting out like drops of hot fat, my brain was telling me to put the phone down but my arm wouldn't do it.

"Maggie? Darling, it's me."

"What do you want?"

"Well, I . . ."

"What can you possibly want?"

"I want you sweetheart."

She started crying, her voice wavering through the ear-piece, "I need you."

"What's to need? What are you talking about?"

"I'm in the hospital Maggie. I need you. Please come."

I took the address, quickly locked the house and ran to her. Ran to the tube. Ran through my tears. Ran straight into it.

I've stopped running now. But then I couldn't help myself, she needed me and I would be there for her. I would stay with her as long as she needed me, like Nancy to Bill Sykes. Only even sicker.

But there's only so much pain that even I could take.

I found her at the Accident and Emergency section of King's College. She said a motorbike had hit her. It looked more like a bus. She said she'd been on her way to her mother's. Came out of the tube, crossed the road and wham! She'd been hit.

As I looked at her I felt like I'd been hit too.

The nurses asking the questions believed her. They probably see a lot of it. Women who've been hit by fast moving vehicles. Or say they have. She told them it had happened the night before, late, the bike hadn't stopped. She said she'd gone home in shock, her own car in the garage, she'd travelled all that way home on the Northern Line, hadn't thought about going to the hospital. Didn't realise she might need to until she saw herself in the mirror and saw what the other late night travellers had been staring at. Until she woke up in the morning crying with pain. She got up and took herself to the hospital. They sent her to X-ray and then said they'd better admit her – "We'll just keep you in today for observation, dear." They wanted to keep an eye on her black eye, possible concussion, sprained ankle, cuts to the face, hands and arms and fractured rib. I offered to take her home, but they said they'd rather keep her in for the night – so much for all those NHS cuts they keep bleating about. I saw her in pain and went into caring mode. Straight into it, like nothing else had happened, like we hadn't been apart at all.

Like we'd never been apart.

She had to talk to a policewoman, gave me as her next of kin, the policewoman just smiled – maybe it was the uniform, but she looked like a dyke to me. The policewoman asked a few questions about the bike, the rider, none of which she could answer.

"I just stepped out and it was there," was all she kept saying. The policewoman took a few notes but didn't seem to take it very seriously.

I wonder how hurt you have to be before they really care. Dead?

I suppose they have that reserve of all medical type people, where once you've seen someone mangled or garotted or shot or something equally hideous, then you're not likely to be impressed by a couple of cracked ribs.

Not like me. I was very impressed indeed.

They cleaned her up and then put her into a thin white bed
in a sterile room with four other women. I stayed with her
as long as I could, but in the late afternoon they made me
go. No pushing, no shoving, just that firm nurse's author-
ity where the uniform does all the talking and you don't
have any room to argue. The nurse was my age or younger,
but it was her world and she held all the power.

"You have to go now dear. Come along. She'll be able to
go tomorrow but for now she needs to rest. Come back in
the morning, she'll be feeling a lot better then and you can
have a proper chat. Off you go."

A proper chat. I couldn't remember the last time we'd had
one of those.

Had it only been weeks or was it years? She smiled at me
from the bed, we'd hardly been able to speak to each other
anyway, there was too much to say and we both knew that
once we started we'd never be able to contain the torrent
of words. We held each other in silence for a few minutes
and then I left. I didn't kiss her. Her face was cut and
bruised anyway and I didn't want to hurt her.

I didn't want to hurt me.

I walked out of the building and up the street, feeling like
I was seeing it for the first time. The street, the trees, the
world. It looked sharp and bright. The year had turned
while I'd been in mourning. And it felt great. Awe-full. For
some reason I was very scared. And very happy. She'd
come back to me. She'd needed me. She'd called me.
Wherever she'd been, she'd needed me in the end. Whoever
she'd been with, it had been me she'd turned to. Me she
trusted. Me she needed to comfort her. I felt like I had an
identity again. Like the little green plastic wristband the

hospital had given her. Hers gave her name and reference number. Mine said "HERS". I walked home revelling in the weak sunshine, swimming in the cold air, my head reeling with the contradictions. It was pointless. And I loved her. She'd treated me appallingly. And she loved me. I hated her. She had lied to me. She had cheated me. And I loved her. It kept coming back to that. That's all it ever came back to.

That's all it ever amounts to. I loved her, therefore I had to be with her.

I love her. Therefore she has to be with me.

I went home. To our home. I pulled the curtains and let in the light. I looked at it. Looked at what my life had become. Five rooms, tastefully furnished. She'd tidied up, kept it all clean and ready. Waiting for me to come home? She'd gone out without turning on the answerphone though, so I couldn't pry into the messages her life had taken since I'd left. There was a pile of mail for me. Mostly letters from the bank, bills, leaflets and publicity for a dozen new plays. A few angry notes from venues where I'd cancelled gigs with little notice. A postcard from my father, staying with my aunt and uncle in Dorset, with love from all three of them and a reminder to call more often. I walked through the flat opening curtains and windows. Into the bedroom, our bedroom. I ignored the bed, pulled open the wardrobe door and stared at my clothes, wondered why it all looked so tidy and then remembered I'd been throwing all the old stuff out when I'd "left home". I felt like a stranger. Like a trespasser.

I made myself a cup of coffee and braced myself to call Dolores. Luckily Keith answered the phone.

"Keith? It's Maggie."

"Where are you? Are you OK?"

"I'm fine. I'm at home."

"Oh?"

"She's home Keith."

"With you now?"

"No. She's in the hospital."

I told him about the accident, about how hurt she looked, how raw. He listened and, because he was not Dolores, he said "All right sweetheart. It's up to you. You know you can come back here if you want to. You know there's plenty of room."

"I know. I just feel that I . . ."

"Ought to give it another go?"

"Yeah, I suppose so, I don't know, I know Dolly'll say I'm an idiot."

"She can talk! You have to do what feels right Maggie. Sometimes you have to do what feels right, even when you know it's not."

"Hey, Keith, how did you get to be so aware?"

"I'm a father and a widower – even politics can't teach you what that's taught me. Look after yourself Mag and call me if you need anything."

We hung up. I finished my coffee thinking about Keith. It was typical really, even when I'd gone out with men they had never been like him. I'd always gone out with the bastards, the good-looking heart breakers. My teenage best friend had always had the "good guys", the ones you could happily take home to your mother – and, of course, she'd always treated them like shit. Gay or straight, the imbalances of love always exist, hiding in the dark corners of rosily lit rooms, waiting to trip you up, knock you over, knock you out.

Just waiting. A silent trap. Sharp pain or orgasm – a scream sounds the same when you open your mouth to let it out.

I went to sleep in our bed that night. Alone but for the shape the sense of her made next to me. Her smell, my left arm lying where her right arm would lie beside it, my left toes stroking the place where the top of her right foot would be. She lay asleep in a hospital bed and I slept with her ghost.

A spirit can be a very comfortable bedfellow.
    As long as you're asleep.

CHAPTER 21

Dream topping

I dreamt about her that night. Dreamt that she was walking towards me stumbling and holding her arms out to me. I'd run to her. She was crying. But just as I reached her and put out my arms to comfort her she'd turn into someone else. Dolores, Annie, Keith, my dad. And they'd laugh at me and push me away, then it would start again. It was on the top of a big cliff and I'd have to run and run to get to her and every time I did she turned into someone else. Then the dream changed again and we were both running through a series of corridors, hospital corridors I think. I don't know what we were running from but I know it was getting closer and closer and I was scared of it. I couldn't run as fast as her and she was ahead of me, pulling me on. Her fingers digging into the flesh of my upper arm, then her grasp slipped and she was holding my wrist, pulling at my wrist, she was hurting me, I couldn't keep up, I screamed at her to let me go and she did, she ran on in front of me, she wouldn't look back and she left me there, in the dark. She just left me.

I woke up scared. Alone and scared. I dressed and practically ran all the way to the hospital, determined to get her out and bring her home and keep her there with me.

I did.

They let her come home with me on the strict instructions that she rest for a week. She'd called her office from the hospital and told them not to expect her in for a while. I took her home and unplugged the telephone. I didn't even want answerphone messages to disturb us. She slept for most of that day, I only went out to get more milk. Late that night, it was a Wednesday, she woke up, wide awake and came into the lounge. She turned the TV off and sat beside me on the sofa.

"I guess I've got some explaining to do, huh?"

"Yeah, you could put it that way."

"I'm going to tell you something. I want you to listen to the whole story before you say anything. OK?"

I nodded and sat down beside her.

She told me it all. How she'd met John a few months after we'd moved in together, just as she was having those initial "Is this it forever, then?" panics. We were going through a bad patch and it was one of those times when all her job had to offer was routine office work. She was bored. So she agreed to meet him for dinner. On a Friday so I wouldn't be suspicious.

"Didn't your parents care?"

"I told them I was working. Work's important to them, you know that."

She had dinner with him the first time, and then a second, that's when she refused to tell him her name. That's when she made up the name. She told him to call her September. Told him it was more exciting that way.

"But why?"

"I don't know. I've always liked make believe."

"But couldn't you have played it with me?"

"No. We had a real life. We have a real life. I didn't want to jeopardize that by playing games with it."

"Well you were playing the bloody olympics with me.

You lied to me."

"I know. I'm sorry."

She liked the mystery of it. The intrigue. It looked like she actually liked having to lie to me. Then she told me about the wig and the contacts. I didn't believe her at first so she got them out of the wardrobe. At the very back, in a small case behind the "maybe" bag that was still waiting to be sorted through. I made her put them on. It was amazing, and I thought I was the actress! Even bruised and tired, the effect was incredible. She looked much more glamorous, not the stunning, sharp beauty I'd first fallen in love with but someone similar, a little softer, a little more "girly".

"One look for the girls and one for the boys, huh?"

"You've got to believe me Maggie, I never had sex with him. I liked him. Liked meeting him, liked being with him. Liked having this sort of 'other life' thing."

"So where does New York fit in?"

"New York?"

She looked surprised.

"In the card, the one dated on my birthday, the one I found, he says 'Hope you had a good time in New York' – what's that then? Somewhere to play at being a redhead?"

"No hon, you're the only redhead in my life. New York was . . . it was just to see if I could do it."

"What?"

"We'd been together ages, right?"

"So?"

"I was feeling restless, scared. I didn't want to break up, but I know what I'm like. I run away. I push people away if they get too close."

"You've only just discovered that?"

"No. But after a while it was starting to scare me. You've always wanted everything to be the same. You want to plan everything forever. That scares me. John was a way of getting round it, but even he was becoming routine. I was bored. No wait! – not bored with you, with us. Bored with me. So I decided to see if I could go away without you knowing."

"And you went to New York?"

"Yeah."

"I don't believe you."

"OK, don't believe me. But it happened. I arranged a courier flight, flew out on Wednesday morning and flew back on Thursday afternoon."

"I'd have known."

"You thought I'd spent the night in Bath with Mr and Mrs Duncan from Indiana. Remember?"

I remembered.

"But you called me from Bath."

"They do have telephones in New York, Maggie."

"Well why didn't you tell me?"

"I meant to, but it was only the week after your birthday and you were so upset with me. I didn't know why. You were just going out to the gym all the time, you wouldn't talk to me. I thought you were seeing someone else."

"Well, what about my birthday? His card was dated the night of my birthday. You told me you sat in the car all night."

"A slight exaggeration. But I didn't lie when I told you I was torn between you and my family. I really was. I hadn't arranged to see John that night. But when we had the fight about it I knew you were right, I couldn't go to my parents. But I knew they were right too, I should be with them to remember my grandmother. So I stayed away from you both. I called him at work and asked him to meet me for a drink."

"And told him all about it I suppose?"

"No. He doesn't know about you."

"What?"

"It's true. I've never spoken to him about you or my family or my work. They were my first rules."

"Oh for God's sake, you're not bloody Mata Hari!"

"I know it sounds pathetic and unbelievable but. . ."

"Where did you meet him?"

"In Waterstones on Kensington High Street."

"What were you doing over there?"

"Waiting for some Americans. I was taking them shopping. He was nice. We were both looking at the Van Gogh books. They had a sale. He offered to buy me a coffee."

She had an answer for everything. But I still didn't understand.

"Stop it. Even if I believe your whole bloody story, which I really don't think I can, I still don't understand why. Why lie to me? Why lie to him? Why?"

"Listen Maggie. It's very hard to explain. I don't have a nice simple reason. I did it because I could."

"Like climbing Mt Everest?"

"Yeah, only without the sherpas. Sweetheart, I love you. I love you very much. But you're a very powerful person. You're used to having things your own way. You don't like things to change. You don't like not knowing about everything. You wanted to know where I was all the time. You couldn't stand it when I went out with my old friends. You wanted me all to yourself. And I needed to keep a bit back for me. I needed to have a piece of me that was only mine."

"So you made her up?"

"Yes. I made her up."

By now it was three o'clock in the morning. I was totally confused. In one way I felt better, closer to her than I had in ages. It seemed like we could maybe even try to have a relationship again. Somehow.

We went to bed, she to our room, me to the sofabed. It was still too uncertain for us to sleep together.

I fell asleep trying to piece it together. Unwilling to disbelieve her, but still feeling a nagging doubt. Some time in the night I woke up with a single clear thought. I know I should have written it down, that's what they always say isn't it? Write it down so you don't forget. But I didn't bother. In the morning it was gone and we tried to carry on.

I know what that thought was now.

If she first met him in Waterstones on Kensington High Street, why was she already wearing the wig and contacts?

As I said, shame I didn't write it down when I first thought of it.

CHAPTER 22

Circuit training

Saz leafed through her copy of *Time Out*. In the Comedy section Maggie Simpson "Loud and sassy comedienne" was down to perform in two well known venues, and in the Gay section she was listed under a benefit for the Hackney Women's Centre. So it was a choice between a venue she'd never been to and probably wouldn't feel too comfortable in as a brand new peroxide blonde, or a place where like as not she'd spend most of the evening trying to avoid catching the eye of various ex-lovers, when she really wanted to have her whole concentration on Ms Simpson. She checked out the other acts – at the Clapham venue on Friday, Maggie was the only woman performing on a bill with one double act, one other stand-up and some "impro" team, while at the Stoke Newington pub on Sunday ("Women Only", of course) she was on with two poets and a folk singer. That decided it. Saz figured even an evening of "Could I have a suggestion of a household item, please?" would be better than two poets and a folk singer, and made plans to hit Clapham on Friday.

Claire called to say that her friend in New York could check up on Calendar Girls, but as it was less than strictly legal it would take some time.

"Listen, Claire. Tell her she's got all the time in the world, but if she can get it done within the week, she's also

got my flat for her own London apartment for any fortnight she'd care to name."

"Where will you go?"

"Probably your floor honey, just tell her."

Suitably prompted, Claire's friend said she could just
about promise copies of deeds and title-holders within four
days. And was the middle of August OK?

By nine o'clock on Friday night the back room of the pub
was pretty full and Saz was beginning to doubt the wisdom
of her choice. The room itself was no worse than hundreds
of other pub rooms – dirty, smoky and aesthetically
nothing. The crowd was fairly ordinary too – there seemed
to be at least two stag party groups, one similarly raucous
group of young women and the rest were in twos and
threes. Not a single person among them. And all were
drinking heavily. Saz had spotted Maggie Simpson when
she came in, she'd been standing at the back of the room
talking to a young guy who later turned out to be the
compère. An Australian, he'd come in for a fair bit of heck-
ling from a couple of the more inebriated young men, but
after a couple of well placed put downs, mostly along the
lines of an Englishman's inability to drink without telling
the whole world about it, he soon had them under control.
The double act were on first. Like all the others, they were
young men and seemed to spend most of the next thirty
minutes abusing each other, much to the delight of the
loud groups of similarly abusive young men. Then Maggie
came on. Saz had to admit that if nothing else she was
brave. And if she hadn't known she was a dyke, she'd never
have guessed. Certainly the boys on the front table
couldn't tell either. The only hints were in a couple of
jokes about "My lover", where there was no specific reference to any form of personal pronoun, and they were far
too obtuse for the boys slavering over her to notice. Once

she'd realised that, Saz saw beyond the obvious meaning in most of Maggie's jokes and ended up enjoying herself more than she'd thought she would. Almost as much as the pissed guys on the front table who'd spent most of Maggie's act trying to matchmake her with the prospective groom.

At the interval Saz went to the bar. She was just about to pay when she caught sight of Maggie to her left. She seemed smaller off stage. Smaller and younger. Saz smiled at her.

"Um, Maggie. I really enjoyed your stuff – can I get you a drink?"

Maggie looked at her. She seemed taken aback at first and then, looking closer at Saz, thanked her.

"Ah, yeah. I'd like a gin and tonic. Please."

"You're very funny."

"Thanks. That's the idea."

"You've got some great material."

"I saw you laughing. You're a good audience."

"I think I got some of the jokes."

"Well, I would hope so."

"No, I mean some of the ones that went over the boys' heads."

"Oh right. Those. Well, they're a pretty straight bunch, but I can usually spot the dykes in the audience – they get the subtle hints."

"Special lesbian code, huh?"

"Something like that."

By the time they were on to their third drink and the worst of the impro was over, the two women were chatting. Not exactly getting on well, Maggie seemed too reserved for that, but at least they were talking. Saz had avoided questions about her own work by saying she was on Enterprise

Allowance, which at least was true. She'd also made clear to Maggie that she was single – and available, but so far the hint had not been taken up. By the end of the night Saz had just about given up on Caroline's lead. Maggie had made not one mention of a girlfriend and from the way she talked it sounded like she lived alone. Then Maggie looked at her.

"Saz, this is going to sound really strange . . ."

"Go ahead."

"Well, your hair, is it natural?"

"God no! It's peroxide. Can't you tell?"

"Yeah, I know it's peroxide – I mean – is it real or is it a wig?"

"Oh. Oh no. It's real, see – doesn't come off."

Saz tugged at her hair.

"Why? Does it look like one?"

"No. Sorry. It's just that – a friend of mine had a similar wig. Same colour. It makes you look a bit like her. I thought you were her at first. From behind. When I saw you standing at the bar. You startled me."

"She doesn't like pubs?"

"No, it's not that, I just wouldn't expect to see her here, that's all." Maggie seemed agitated and very glad to see a large man coming towards her.

"Oh, Chris. Great. Got lots of cash for me then have you?"

"Not bad. Good night tonight love. Have I booked your next spot?"

"In a couple of months I think."

"Good, well done. Glad you're back. We missed you."

"Thanks Chris. Well, Saz. Got my money, time to go. Been nice talking to you, thanks for the drink."

"Ah yeah. Look, could we meet again some time?"

"I don't think so. I'm not really free. But thanks anyway."

With that, she picked up her bag and practically ran out of the room.

At home Saz called Caroline.

"And James hasn't tried to contact you?"

"Well, if he has, he'll only get an unobtainable tone."

"Was there enough money for the phone?"

"Plenty, you're also paying for my dinner tonight, thank you."

"Good, very nice of me."

She told her about meeting Maggie.

"Well, they definitely used to go out together and she obviously knows about Calendar Girls if she knows about the wig."

"Not necessarily, she could just have seen September in it. For a fancy dress or something. I think, given how much we know of September's lying or fantasising with John Clark, we can't just assume she'd tell her girlfriend all about it."

"Yes, but while she may have lied to Clark, she might have been totally honest with Maggie."

"Sure. Really. Would you like your girlfriend working there? Besides that, if September was running coke or whatever it is from the States, and you were Maggie, would you go out to grotty clubs to be funny for nasty drunken youths for a mere eighty quid?"

"Depends. Maybe she likes grotty clubs."

"She seemed pretty eager to get out of there tonight."

"Or eager to get away from you?"

"Thanks."

"Maybe she's suffering from Protestant work ethic."

"Half her stand-up routine's about being Catholic."

"Well – how's this? She felt too guilty spending September's ill-gotten gains and determined to earn her own money."

"No. It's something else. She looked really scared when she first saw me at the bar. She went white."

"As a ghost?"

"No. More like she'd just seen one."

"Careful!"

"Oh come on Carrie, she's hardly an ice-pick wielding dyke!"

"Ice-pick wielding dykes don't kill each other, remember?"

"Oh yeah, I forgot. Silly me. But short of going round to her place and forcing her to let me in on the hunt for the elusive September, what can I do?"

"Talk to Annie about her."

"I hardly know Annie."

"I do. She's nice. Talk to her. You'll find a way, you're the detective. And give her my love."

"Oh? Is she someone else from your past? Someone you maybe 'forgot' to tell me about?"

"She's not. But her brother is."

CHAPTER 23

Sweeties for the car

The next few days were difficult. It was sharp, our "relationship", like walking barefoot on frost. I waited for it to pass. We were new again, scratchy. And polite, we were very polite.

"Morning."

"Morning."

"Would you like a cup of tea?"

"Oh no. It's fine, I can make my own."

"Really, it's no bother."

"Well, if you're sure. . ."

"You do have sugar don't you?"

"Ah, yes. Yes, thanks."

We were like new flatmates before the first fight about who'd finished the milk.

It was OK in a way though. I think we both felt chastened. Calm after a night of rain. We wanted to try again. At least we looked like we did. I did. I wanted to find a new way to make it work. If such a way existed. And I think we would have too. If they'd just have left us alone.

But people never do, do they? They're always there. Looking over your shoulder. The only time they leave you alone is when you really need them. When the night terrors hit and you wake alone. Covered in cold sweat and crying out for a hand to soothe you. That's when they leave you alone.

And then he arrived. I guess I first saw him a couple of weeks ago. Monday, maybe Sunday. He was sitting in a red car parked near our flat. Round the corner. I noticed the car first. Expensive looking. American or European – left hand drive. I don't suppose I thought anything about him until I realised he was still there three days later. He looked expensive too. I couldn't have said then if he was tall or not. I only saw him sitting in the front of his car. Smoking. He was quite good-looking I suppose, if you like that kind of man. Clean cut, square jaw, fair. My mother would have called him a "matinee idol". Too good to be true if you ask me.

It didn't occur to me that he mattered. He was just a bloke in a car.

We were getting on all right. We were wary and careful of each other. Still sleeping apart. It seemed more sensible. Though she crept into my bed late at night a couple of times – sort of sexual, sort of just warm. We tried to have sex once, but I couldn't come and after a while of trying I told her it was OK, maybe tomorrow. She drifted off to sleep and I lay there a long time listening to her breathing. It sounded the same as it always had. Like her lungs couldn't tell what a state my heart was in. We'd have long, late night conversations about "our relationship". I'd always promised myself I'd never do that. Never "work at" a relationship. I'd thought that if it didn't work of its own accord, I'd just walk away. But now, though staying with her seemed marginally less difficult, walking away seemed impossible. We were tied up, tied together. We owned furniture. Separating a record collection is easy. You can always make a tape of the Tracy Chapman. How do you share out a sofa-bed?

I remember I went to a gig on the Thursday night. I left about eight and he was still sitting there, car parked under a streetlight, reading *The Standard*. Looking back on it, his interest in *The Standard* seemed a little too avid for such a lightweight paper. But I didn't know how tall he was then. I didn't know much at all. He wasn't there when I came back just after midnight.

I told her about him. Just mentioned this bloke in a car.
  She nearly hit the roof.
  "Where? Where is he?"
  "I don't know. Gone home I 'spose."
  "Is he still there?"
  "No. I told you. He was there earlier. He's not there now."
  "What did he look like?"
  "I don't know."
  "You must know."
  "Calm down sweetheart."
  "What?"
  "It's only a man in a car."
  "No it's not."
  "Oh right, what is it then?"
  "You don't understand."
  "Yep, I don't. What the hell are you talking about?"
  "Christ!"
  "What's the matter?"
  "Where's his car?"
  "I don't know, it was just around the corner."
  "But not now?"
  "No. Maybe he'll be there again tomorrow."

"Damn it! Why didn't you tell me sooner?"

"I didn't know you cared! Look, what the fuck is your problem?"

"I . . . I. Oh nothing. Nothing."

"Nothing my big fucking toe."

"Don't shout at me."

"I am not shouting." I whispered "Tell me what you're talking about."

"No."

"Tell me what you're talking about."

"It doesn't matter. It's probably not even him."

"Who?"

"No-one. Forget it."

"Who? Is it your Mr Clark?"

"No. 'My' Mr Clark looks nothing like your idea of a matinee idol."

"Well who then?"

She wouldn't say. Refused to talk about it. Wouldn't even let me bring the subject up. But I know she didn't sleep that night. I heard her prowling the room all night. I heard her because I didn't sleep either. He was there again the next morning, Friday, but not in the evening. I didn't see him for the next few days. We got some sleep.

Things improved. After about a week we realised we could argue again without the house crumbling around us. It got back to normal.

Whatever normal is.

We went shopping together. Like any other happy couple touring the aisles of Sainsburys. Looking for the other gay couples – easy to spot, their hands only just touching as they steered the trolleys together. The lesbians mostly in the direction of the pulses and the grains and as far from

the fresh meat as possible, the gays over to the Lean
Cuisine fridge. Stereotyping I know, but I can't help it if
my local supermarket attracts the more traditional family.

She didn't contact John Clark. Said she'd just cut him off.
It would be easier that way. She wouldn't have to do any
explaining. I thought it would probably worry him sick –
but didn't feel kindly enough towards him to mention it.
Her mother called but she left the message unanswered. I
said she should go over if she wanted to. That I'd be all
right with it. She said she'd rather not. She wanted to
spend time with me, with no interruptions. She went back
to work for a couple of days and then asked if she could
have some time to sort herself out, told them she was still
feeling pretty shaky after the accident. She wasn't due any
time off, so they gave her two weeks "compassionate
leave". That is, without pay.

What happens if it's uncompassionate? Do you have to pay
them?

On the Monday of the first week we stayed inside all day.
It was cold outside and grey. We watched daytime TV and
ate tomato soup. We sat together on the sofa in our night-
time T-shirts. We held hands for the first time in days. That
night she kissed me goodnight. Calling goodnight just like
the Waltons. Just like.

The next day we went up to the women's pond at
Hampstead. It was wonderful. That space, full to over-
flowing in summer was virtually empty. Just us and a
couple of the old ladies – the ones who swim every day of
the year. The ones who break the ice so they can go in. The
ones who call it the "Ladies' Pond". It was one of those
rare beautiful winter days – high blue sky, crisp breeze,

and cold and clear so that it sorts your brain out. We had a picnic. Summer sandwiches while wrapped up in thick jumpers and blanket. I was almost tempted to swim myself, but she persuaded me that the "ladies" wouldn't approve of me going swimming in my bra and knickers.

My bra and her knickers. Our clothes were mixed up again.

We spent most of the daylight out in the world and then came home as it was getting dark. I spotted his car as we turned the corner but didn't say anything to her. We'd had too nice a day to spoil it by bringing Mr Mystery into it.

Well, that's what I thought then. Of course, after all that, it was me who spoilt it. Fucked it up just as completely as if we'd never got back together in the first place. Only worse. It was just a couple of weeks ago. I wish I'd never seen him.

But we did have a lovely day.

CHAPTER 24

Exercising BT

At three thirty on Tuesday morning Saz was woken by the phone. She rolled out of bed and reached for where it lay under a pile of clothes. She finally pulled out both the handpiece and a dirty sock.

"Yeah?"

"Saz. It's Claire."

"Uh-huh?"

"Look, I know it's late but I thought you'd want to know as soon as possible."

"You've fallen in love again?"

"Come on! Even I wouldn't call you about something as trivial as that at three in the morning. No, I just had a call from Sandra in New York – she didn't know how late it was here, it's still a respectable hour there, not that she'd know the meaning of the word."

Saz suddenly felt wide awake. She flicked on the light.

"Claire, don't tell me the history of Greenwich Mean Time, just tell me the story."

"All right then. He's here."

"Who?"

"Your Simon James – real name Simon James McAuley."

"He's where?"

"In London."

"Yes! That's his name, McAuley?"

"Apparently. Not a lot of imagination huh? Just got rid of the last name and uses his first two. He's a very well known businessman in New York. Reputable even. Mixes with all the right people."

"Yeah, I've served most of them champagne – lots of other very well known and equally bent businessmen in New York."

"Maybe, but Sandra says that as far as her department is concerned he's as clean as the driven snow."

"Claire, it's too late for druggy puns."

"It's too early, I didn't even realise it was one."

"Get on with it."

"That's it really, she hasn't got an ounce of dirt on him, though she did say that she met him once at some benefit or something like that and wouldn't trust him with her Rottweiler!"

"Yeah, well, he's not much of a dog lover. How long has he been here?"

"Since the weekend. He's staying in his London flat. In Fulham. Get this – above his London business."

"A business?"

"Handmade, expensive furniture. Viscount Linley kind of stuff."

"He makes furniture?"

"No. The staff make the furniture. He makes money by selling it to silly rich people who think one chair's worth several thousand quid – even without a royal name on it."

"He's got a business in London?"

"Saz, I know it's late but there's no need to keep repeating everything I say. She said he makes a trip over here about once every eighteen months. 'To check up on his business'."

"How did you get all this?"

"Sandra's office. She's very well informed. And she has a tax department connection."

"The old lesbian mafia huh?"

"No. Sandra's straight. It's her husband."

"Same idea. And?"

"Well, Mr McAuley makes money here so he has to declare it for tax over there or he'd never be able to use it would he? And that's how they know about the business."

"How long has it been going?"

"Since the mid eighties."

"And Calendar Girls?"

"March 1981. Calendar Girls in New York came first, he made his money there, followed it up by expanding into business in London."

"What's it called?"

"You're gonna love this. Miss September."

"God, I might have guessed – all English girls."

"What?"

"Nothing. Just something he told me. Now why would he have a furniture business here?"

"Maybe they don't have much money to spend on 'furniture d'art' in Arkansas. They're probably not ardent royalists. I don't know. Because he wanted to. Because it was there."

"No, what I mean is, if he was going to expand, why have a different type of business? Calendar Girls does very well in New York. I'm sure he could get the same thing going here."

"Maybe he just likes chairs?"

"Very plausible. No. Everyone knows how prohibitive business taxes can be in Britain."

"Only you darling, the rest of us don't have quite such a caring relationship with our local Small Business Officers."

"Claire, you've got a big fat job with a major law firm with offices in three central city locations – I'm surprised you even know that Enterprise Allowance exists."

"I didn't, you told me about it. Anyway I'm sure he's clever enough to get round something as minor as taxes."

"Of course he can, but I can't believe it's a real business. It's got to have something to do with whatever September was carrying for him."

"Heavy trade in smuggled Chippendale legs, maybe?"

"No. The drugs or whatever it is are coming from New York, not going there."

"Well in that case, perhaps the chairs are worth four thousand quid after all."

"What?"

"Chippendale legs."

"Claire, it's quarter to four in the morning. Talk sense."

"Hollow legs, Saz. Easily filled with a certain fine white powder."

"You think so? Bit obvious isn't it?"

"Well, you didn't get it. I don't know, but it sounds about as likely as all the rest of this. Gambling, disguises, drugs – are you sure you know what you're doing?"

"More or less. Anyway, it's September I'm worried about. Look, thanks for this Claire. It's really useful. Give me the details and I'll get on to it in the morning."

Saz put the telephone down and tried to go back to sleep. After about an hour she gave up, dressed and went for a run. By the time she got back, showered and breakfasted it was six thirty and just about feasible that she could ring Helen and Judith. Judith answered the phone.

"Yes?"

"It's Saz, did I wake you?"

"No, but you did disturb us."

"At six thirty in the morning? You are eager."

"Helen had something important on, she only got in half an hour ago. What can we do for you?"

Saz told them what she knew about James and Helen got on the other phone.

"Listen, you don't have proof of any of this do you?"

"No. It's all suspicion. And hearsay. And interpretation – he says 'pigeon', I assume drugs. Not an altogether extravagant assumption, given the coke in his desk drawer."

"Right, cos if you did have proof, I'd have to go official with it."

"I know that, but then he'd know someone was after him."

"Can't be helped. If you're right, I expect there's quite a few people after him. Look, the best we can do is check on the records, see if this London business is legit, what he's got it registered as. That kind of thing. Jude can check his status with immigration."

"Thanks."

"No problem, but you don't have much time."

"What do you mean?"

"Listen Saz, we're both good little police girls who want to be big important police ladies and unfortunately neither of us are masons. We can't keep things quiet for long. Someone's bound to want to know why we're asking, and we have a – a 'duty' – for want of a much better word, to tell them. Your job is to find Miss September, the woman I mean, it sounds like it might be a police job to deal with Mr James."

"McAuley."

"Yeah, him. But he isn't your problem. And you shouldn't make him your problem either. Got it?"

"I understand, how long can you give me?"

"A couple of days maximum, then you'll have to come and talk to someone and we'll start something official. All right?"

"Yeah, 'spose so. You'll let me know what you find out?"

"Soon as. Can we get back to our other business now?"

"Yeah, go for it. Thanks."

Saz put the answerphone on and went back to bed. She woke in time to speak to Helen at midday who said that Simon James McAuley had a perfect record both as a citizen and a tax payer and had flown into Heathrow on Saturday morning, declaring his intention to stay in the country for two weeks – to check on his business and to holiday.

"He's good at his job Saz, I'll give him that. Mr McAuley has never had the slightest problem with our boys, his staff of four are all highly qualified, very respectable – one manager, two cabinet makers and a secretary and every one of them pays their poll tax. I mean council tax. Or whatever it's called now. They pay it."

"OK big sister. Thanks for letting me know."

"I do have some good news for you though."

"What's that? Judith told her parents?"

"Yeah really, and the Pope just married Mother Theresa. No, something much more pertinent – Annie Cox is looking for a lodger."

"Police computers told you that?"

"No, you silly tart – *Capital Gay*, Accommodation Offered."

"So?"

"So, now you've got the perfect excuse to see her. Not only do you have a mutual friend, you're also dying to move into her house."

"Thanks Hells. Inspector Morse has nothing on you."

"I should hope not. Can't stand bloody opera."

Saz called Annie, mentioning both Caroline and the ad, and was promptly invited that afternoon for tea.

"Yes thanks Annie, I will have a slice of that lovely home-made gingerbread, and the name of Maggie Simpson's girl-friend – if you don't mind."

CHAPTER 25

Things go better with coke

Then everything happened very quickly. It was like the Christmas rush. Suddenly it creeps up on you and you find there's hundreds of things you've forgotten. You're not quite ready. You want to ask for just two more days. But you know they'd never give them to you.

Our first Christmas together had been amazing. Initially she'd been dead against our acknowledging it at all. No fir tree had ever decorated the hallowed halls of her mezuzah-protected abode. I told her Jesus was Jewish. She said a hanukiah would be pretty dangerous among all that straw in the stable. I explained that any teenage girl who could persuade her fiancé she'd been impregnated by the Holy Spirit could probably cope with the lack of a fire extinguisher. She still wasn't convinced, so I explained the pagan roots of the festival and how Jesus was probably born in April anyway. Like most semi-Christians, I'm much better at explaining when Jesus was probably born, than how he came to be born at all. Besides which, how could such an influential man possibly be a Capricorn? No, he had to be April and Arian. (Though obviously not Aryan – I took pains to spell the word out loud.) Pagan festival established, we set to it with a will.

Tree, presents, mistletoe – all to my own family's ritual specifications. No arguments here about what order things went, who did what. Not for us the endless rounds of – "Well, we always give out the presents in the morning" … "But my mother always makes her own brandy butter!"

A week before Christmas it was ready and we ran outside to look up at our handiwork. There in the big window of our second floor flat it blazed. Christmas tree with four different strands of electric light blinking on and off in syncopated time with the flickering candles of the hanukiah. Natural light and man-made light. Man made Light. Light made Man. The Catholic metaphor was lost on her.

For our Christmas breakfast we ate smoked salmon and latke. We began our lunch with chicken soup and ended it with plum pudding. And ate prawn crackers while we watched Dorothy fall asleep in the poppy field. Will that girl never learn?

This year our concession to the birthday festival was a sprig of mistletoe above the door in the hall. We didn't want to make too much of a fuss about it, we just needed some time. To see if we could get together again. Or if we were destined to be flatmates forever. She still didn't want to go back to work so I rang around a few places, left messages to say I was available to fill in for last minute cancellations. I waited for the phone to ring. And even dared to answer it. Lucky her mother didn't call.

And the work rolled in. There's always lots of work at this time of year. People want to be cheered up. They want to forget it's cold and dark outside.

I know I do.

I came home late on Monday night. This Monday, the one just gone. After a gig. It was raining. His car was parked in the same place. Pissed me off. I hadn't seen him for a few days and I thought maybe he'd gone away. I decided I'd had enough. A couple of beers and a good night's work, applause still ringing in my ears had fired me up. I went up to the car. To tell him to go away. Whoever he was looking for wasn't going to be coming out of Grange House at almost two o'clock in the morning. Only he wasn't in the car. It was empty.

I was about to put my key in the door lock when I heard him. A man's voice, raised, angry. And her – scared. I was trying to listen even as I was fumbling with the lock. I ran through the hall and into the kitchen. She was sitting at the kitchen table, her head in her hands. She looked like she'd been crying for hours. He was standing over her.

"Who the fuck are you?"

He looked up as I reached for the knife drawer. It was him. The man from the car. Not that I was really surprised. I'd almost expected him. He smiled at me but kept his hand tight on her shoulder.

"Come on September, introduce me to your little friend." The bastard had an American accent, she just kept crying.

"Who the fuck are you?"

"Maggie, just leave it. He was just going."

"What? No English hospitality? No cup of tea?"

She stood up and shook herself free of his hand.

"Simon, piss off. There's a witness here now. You can't possibly deal with both of us. Just go."

He stood there for a minute, like he was weighing up her words. Then he just smiled at me, turned, stroked her hair and kissed her on the forehead. She let him. She was very scared.

"Bye – ah – Maggie was it? Been nice meeting you."

"Fuck off."

"Charmed, I'm sure. Well, no doubt I'll see you later. There's a little unfinished business to deal with."

And he left. Sauntered out the door like a Sunday afternoon stroll. He stopped just by the mistletoe in the hall, looked up at it and down at me. I reached past him and ripped it off the wall. I slammed the door and double locked it after him.

Back in the kitchen she was crying. Sobbing. And shaking. She was a real mess. I made tea, hot and sweet like on telly, wrapped her in a blanket and waited. It came out bit by bit. The place in New York. How she'd met him through a client, not long before she'd met me. It was like the John Clark thing. It appealed to her sense of mystery. She said for a long time it had only been the hostessing, but then one time when she'd really needed some money he'd asked her about taking some stuff to London for him. And she'd agreed. It was in an ornament. An ugly ornament like the ones she'd sometimes have around our place. She said it wasn't at all safe, but that was part of it. The excitement. Her safe life with her parents, the safe mapped-out future they'd had for her – she said it was a way of subverting it – but without ever having to confront them. Sort of like being in the Resistance – only the cause was herself. And she'd been running these two other strands quite separately, except where one provided an excuse for the other. It was hard to believe. I'd swallowed the Clark story even where it was being a cover for this one. There were so many lies.

Too many lies.

But she didn't see it like that. She thought it was exciting. The drugs thing scared me, I didn't see how she could do it so much and get away with it, but she said she'd probably only carried drugs for two or three of the fifteen or so New York trips she'd made. All of the others were clean and the customs people began to recognise her, used to wave her through. Besides, she was so often at the airport, to pick up clients, parties of tourists. Sometimes they took the stuff from her. Sometimes they were real tourists. Sometimes they weren't. I made more tea.

"Why didn't you tell me?"

"I knew you'd hate it."

"Oh? Whatever gave you that idea? Cocaine, hostessing – just the sort of thing I'm really happy for you to be doing. Clever you – you're right. I hate it."

"And I didn't want to stop."

"Not even for me?"

"Not even for myself."

"You're mad."

"I know."

"So what does he want?"

"He thinks I owe him some money."

"Do you?"

"Sort of. I mean someone else really owes him the money, but he doesn't believe me."

"What?"

"The accident – it wasn't an accident. I'd handed the stuff over like I was supposed to, only this time they wanted to pay me."

"Don't they usually?"

"God no. It's too much money. It goes through someone else, or a business. I'm not sure, I only deliver. Anyway, it's got nothing to do with me."

"Only this time it did?"

"Yeah, they gave me the money – cash. I told them I couldn't take it, but they said that if I didn't then they'd never get around to paying. So I took it. It wasn't like I had a choice. Two hundred yards down the road I was knocked over by a motorbike. The 'nice' rider came to help me and took the cash. He knew where to get it from. He'd seen me put it in my bag ten minutes earlier."

"I don't get it. You put all that money away where someone could see you?"

"Yeah. In the house where they gave it to me. He was one of them. Watched me leave the house, got on his bike and knocked me over. Then he comes over to help – looks like he's being a good samaritan and going through my bag to get my name, when actually he's taking the money. Then he goes off to call an ambulance. Only he doesn't come back."

"You should have got someone to stop him."

"Oh yeah, right. 'No luv, don't mind my bruises and broken ribs, just stop that man from stealing from me. Yes, that's right, the man who just nearly killed me.' Yeah, that'd really work."

"Well, why didn't you tell the police?"

"What?"

"The truth."

"That I'm a drug smuggler who needs help? Don't be stupid – they don't let you have secret Friday night dinners in Holloway. No, I worked it out for myself. I knew Simon would want the money and I arranged to borrow it from John. Or I figured I might offer to work at the club – for free, he could keep all my tips, I knew it would take a while but I'd do it eventually. And I'd tell him I wanted out of the couriering thing."

"You borrowed the money from John Clark?"

"Yes. That's what I said."

"So why didn't you give it to him then? To the American?"

"I was going to. But I wanted to talk to him first. Tell him I wanted to stop. Explain that I'd had enough. That this time was the last I'd carry for him. He didn't want to hear that. We'd had a big fight about it already – in New York. He wouldn't listen. And I don't even know if he believed me about the bike rider or not. But I wouldn't be surprised if he already knew about it. Probably arranged it all himself as a way of making me stay with him. Anyway, that's what we were fighting about when you came in."

"Couldn't you have phoned him? Did he have to come all the way from New York for you to tell him you're quitting?"

"He's in London on business. He has a business here too."

"How convenient for him. And how nice of you to invite him over."

"I'm not that stupid. He found out about the accident and got our address from the hospital."

"They're not allowed to give out information like that."

"You're not allowed to bring twelve ounces of cocaine into England hidden in a toy model of the Brooklyn Bridge either. People do."

"Didn't you get paid for all this drug smuggling?"

"Don't call it that, it only happened a few times."

"It's still illegal."

"Yeah sweetheart, so's smoking dope and you've done that often enough."

"It's hardly in the same league. You must have been paid for it."

"Yes."

"Well?"

"It went on flights back to New York. On our trips away, on presents for you – that rather nice antique silver ring you're wearing for instance. It just went, all right? It went, money does. Now I'm practically broke, I've got to get this money to Simon and then find a way of paying John back."

"How much did you borrow from him?"

"Too much."

"Where is it?"

"In the bedroom. Between the mattress and the base. My side of the bed. Anyway, it doesn't make any difference, he'll come back for the money but he's not going to let me go."

"Don't be daft, this isn't the movies. In real life things like this get sorted out."

"In real life people get killed for being late with payments."

"In Columbia maybe."

It went on for hours. Question, answer. Question, answer. Me trying to make it sound less scary than it was, both of us jumping at any sound outside. I couldn't believe she'd been doing all this and I'd known nothing. But then it seemed I'd missed most things anyway. I realised we'd both been leading pretend lives. Hers and the "excitement" factor and mine with my belief that everything could be perfect if only we tried hard enough. Loved hard enough. We were standing in the lounge, watching the winter sun come up around the corner of the block opposite us and I had a sudden thought. A thought about how you can't ever really know anyone. About how hard it is to even know yourself. About how easy it is to lie. And I asked her.

"Did you ever sleep with him?"

"Who?"

"The American."

"Yes."

"Since me?"

"Yes."

I hit her. Just picked up my hand and hit her. Across the head. And as she fell – I watched it, watched it like it was in slow motion, frame by frame. I watched her crack her head on the side of the mantelpiece. I heard her crack her head on the side of the mantelpiece. On the side of the cast iron mantelpiece it had taken us three days to strip. Strip down to the iron. Hard, cold iron. She fell on to the floor. It was eight o'clock in the morning.

I ran out of the door, not stopping to double-lock it. I walked around town for the day. Just walking. I stopped once for a cup of coffee – McDonalds I think, or Burger King – one of those horrible places anyway, where even your coffee smells of ground beef. It had been dark for a long time by the time I came home. I think it was about nine or ten. She was still there but when I looked in the bedroom the bed was all messed up and the money was gone. She lay where she'd fallen that morning. Only now she was cold.

Now she is cold.

CHAPTER 26

Bike races

Saz was halfway through her third cup of tea before the subject of Maggie was even raised. She'd looked all through the house – the spare room, the one she was "interested" in, she'd met Keith's kids as they ran out of the door to a party – and pretended delight at the prospect of sharing a house with three teenagers.

"No really, it's brilliant – you just never meet young people otherwise, do you?"

She'd looked at the garden – ad nauseum – Annie had told her the latin name of almost every plant there, not to mention their planting dates, the likely time of maturity and how she'd cook them. Saz admired the holly bushes and "organic" Christmas tree. She'd been so enthusiastic about the garden that Annie had even threatened to take her to their allotment until Saz confessed she was "dying for a cup of tea" and followed Annie inside, assured of a night suffering from more hayfever than she'd had since she'd been forced on a nature ramble in the third year. And over tea, no gingerbread, just Annie's homemade fruit muffins, she'd managed to discuss Caroline with Keith.

"Oh, it was just a small fling really, hardly a relationship at all. It was not long after my wife had died, I was grasping at straws. We were together for about two months when Carrie decided she really was gay after all and I realised that a bit of grief was in order."

"Grief for Carrie?"

"No, grief for my wife."

"Oh, sorry. Mind you, I don't think it's just her sexuality, Carrie has trouble enough deciding to stay in the same place for three months, let alone with the same person."

"Yeah, well, she's young still, maybe she'll grow out of it."

The kitchen door slammed and Dolores streamed into the room, dressed completely in various shades of pink – bright pink gingham skirt, faded pink silk shirt and pale pink tights thrust into monkey boots – painted white with fluorescent pink flowers.

"Grow out of what?"

"Interrupting other people's conversations hopefully." Annie gave her a kiss.

"Darling this is Saz Martin – she's come to look at the room."

"Oh, right. Hi Saz."

"Hello."

"Are you a dyke?"

"Dolores!"

"It's OK – if she is she'll be charmed by my candour and if she isn't, then she'll know what to expect from at least a third of our friends."

"Yes, I am gay."

"Good guess huh? Mind you, things were so much clearer when lesbians wore the uniform."

Annie pulled Dolores down by the long pink scarf she wore round her ponytail.

"You can talk! Ms Femme Fatale. And anyway, as I only advertised the room in *Capital Gay*, an advert that you paid for, it hardly counts as a good guess on your part, does it? Now shut up and be nice to our guest. You could put the kettle on if you want."

Dolores jumped up from her knee.

"Can't, I've got to get changed, I promised Maggie I'd go round and see her."

Saz suddenly became very quietly interested in her tea cup.

"Why, have you spoken to her?"

"You know I haven't, not for ages anyway, I've tried calling her but there's never any reply and I'm sick of leaving messages on the answerphone. However, I did say I'd go over some time and this is the first night that I've had free and according to *Time Out* – she's free too."

Saz looked up.

"Your friend lists her free evenings in *Time Out*?"

"No, she's a stand up, you might have seen her – Maggie Simpson?"

"Oh yeah, I saw her a few days ago actually. She was really funny. We had a drink together."

"You were drinking together?"

"Well, just one."

"Brilliant! Did she like you?"

"I don't know." Saz looked confused, the conversation wasn't going anywhere near September.

"Dolly!"

"See Annie? Now if Maggie likes Saz . . ."

"Dolores! Maggie already has a girlfriend. Just leave them alone."

Keith poured Saz another cup of tea.

"Annie's right Dol, stay out of it."

"Well it can't hurt just to take Saz with me can it?"

"I'm sure Saz has got a lot more interesting things to do than tagging along with you. Anyway, maybe she's got a girlfriend of her own."

"Have you?"

"Ah, no, actually. I haven't."

"Are you looking?"

"Not really. Sorry. Look, I don't want to be a bother, and it's probably time I left anyway."

"Well, where do you live?"

"Camberwell, why?"

"That's settled then. Maggie lives in Stockwell, I'll take you home via her place. Goody, I'm going to get changed."

Dolores ran upstairs and the next thing they heard was the slamming of several doors and cupboards.

"Ah yes – another dressing trauma. It's traditional around here. For her anyway. Sorry about that Saz," Annie started to clear away the tea things. "Dolores used to go out with Maggie and she still feels very responsible for her. Maggie's had a bit of a hard time with her girlfriend recently and Dol has this idea of finding her someone else."

"What she doesn't appreciate is that they love each other, even with all the crap they've had, I think those two are going to be together forever. I can't see Maggie ever letting her go."

Dolores strode back into the room and threw her arms around Annie, nearly causing her to drop the three tea cups she was taking to the sink.

"That Keith, is merely a myth maintained by one who believes in true love. Which as we all know is completely unobtainable – unless you happen to be called Dolores and Annie!"

Her hair was scraped off her face. New, even thicker black lines prowled under her eyes and she was dressed from head to toe in a black cat suit and black leather boots and jacket. She looked stunning.

"Look at you, you big butch thing."

"Now, now, brother-in-law, don't display your jealousy. You know I always dress down to cross the river. Coming Saz?"

Saz, spotting the best opportunity she'd seen in ages, readily agreed to the visit. She arranged to call Annie the next day muttering nice things about the house and about having to "think it over".

"Yeah fine, it's a shame that you've met Dolly now, Keith and I were hoping she'd stay out until we persuaded you to move in. Anyway, give me a call if she hasn't done too much damage and let me know what you think."

Saz followed Dolores out to the street where she was confronted by her transport – a gleaming Harley. Dolores threw a helmet at her and shouted,

"Get on! This is my favourite part of the day. Early evening sunset, cold wind – we'll be there in no time."

Saz sat behind Dolores on the bike, clutching at the leather thing in front of her as they roared through various side streets and across the river, sun just setting in the bend at Westminster and the wind sculpture on top of the NFT glowing like a beacon at the entrance to the South. When she got off the bike Saz reflected that while they did indeed get to Maggie's flat in no time, she'd also had no time to ask anything about the elusive September, let alone her real name. She followed Dolores up the steps of the Georgian house, two baskets of well nurtured geraniums hanging on either side of the door.

"Is this a housing association place?"

"No. Good old-fashioned private sector – Maggie's girlfriend has expensive tastes."

"Must be hard for Maggie to keep up with?"

"I don't know, but they seem to do very well – they've got all the 'things'! Right, they're on the second floor so she'll have to come down to let us in."

Just as Dolores put up her hand to ring the bell, the door opened. Maggie was obviously just leaving.

"Fuck! You scared me! What are you doing here?"

"Just come for the visit, babe. This is Saz, she said she met you the other day?"

"Oh yeah, ah – at a gig?"

"Yeah, I don't mean to barge ..."

"Look, I've got to go out, I wasn't expecting anyone – I can't ... I've got to get some milk."

"It's OK, we'll wait."

"No, I ... You can't."

"Perhaps you'd rather just see Dolores, I can go home, it's fine." Saz started to walk away.

"No, I don't want to see Dolores, I don't want to see anyone. Leave me alone. Go away. Leave us alone."

Maggie started crying. Not normal crying, not the crying that went with her agitated words but a sort of soft moaning. She slid down the side of the door and Dolores caught her just before she fell to the floor. They held her between them and walked her up the stairs, Dolores alternating between comforting Maggie and abusing her for being so heavy. They went through the door to Maggie's flat and Saz was blasted by the shock of cold air that came at her.

"This way Saz, this is her place, and through to the lounge, that's it, just here."

She pushed open the door to the lounge.

"God, Maggie, it's bloody freezing in here. What's happened, had the power cut off?"

But Maggie was in no state to answer her. The closed curtains were little protection against the cold wind blowing in from the open windows behind them and other than the little amount of street light, the room was very dark.

"The light's over there, on the table. You get it, I'll hold her."

Maggie was still moaning slightly when Saz flicked the switch. She turned back to help Dolores.

Dolores who was white as a sheet and looked like she too was about to faint.

Saz followed the line of her stare to the armchair where she came face to face with September.

CHAPTER 27

Hoarding

And so we've just been staying in together. Me and the woman I live with. The Woman with the Kelly McGillis body. We don't go out, it's cold and dark outside anyway. There's no point.

It's cold and dark inside too.

I stopped answering the phone, and once the tape was used up, I just unplugged the answer machine and let it ring.

We sit here together, but she won't speak to me. As if it's my fault. She's trying to make me feel guilty. And I do.

Catholicism is so similar to Judaism. As my mother's friend Lorna used to say "There's only a page between them."
 Neither of us have ever read much.
 Sometimes I try to get up. Out and about. And I think I should tell someone, but I don't know who to tell. She didn't want anyone to know about that man. Or what she was doing. She didn't want anyone to know, so I don't know who to call.

The phone keeps ringing. It's probably her mother. She can't have spoken to her for weeks now. But if I pick it up,

I'll have to speak to her. And I know she wouldn't want that. Neither of them would want that. And I feel like I'm on my best behaviour now, I have to be, I can't do anything worse. I can't make it any better either.

It's very quiet here now. When the phone's not ringing. Very quiet. No sounds of us arguing. No sounds of us making love.

I picked her up from the floor, I didn't think she'd want to lie there. She was heavier than I thought she'd be. Heavier than the last time I picked her up. Carried her in my arms. There was some stuff, where she'd been lying. Like she'd thrown up. But not much. I tidied it up. Tidied her up. And there was some powder. Coke I suppose. I don't know. I don't know about these things. She knows about these things. They just happen on the TV I think. Not really. I don't know about the drug stuff. It passed me by. I only like beer. And gin, but only with lots of tonic and ice. I tidied it up. I want to tidy it all away. Put it all away. But I know I can't. I have to do something. Tell someone.

It was very cold when I woke up this morning. I don't know how long I've been asleep. I can't tell any more. I'm going to keep the curtains closed from now on. I don't want him to come back. He messed up the bedroom when he was here before. He messed up our lovely bed. I don't think I'll sleep in it again. He's got his money now. He should just go away. But I don't know if he will.

I saw a funny thing this morning. I didn't notice it before. She's not wearing any shoes. And she was. When she fell. When I hit her. When I made her fall.

Fall from grace. Goodbye paradise.

When I ran out of the room – she was wearing shoes. And now she's not. I don't know why. Maybe he wanted to see her feet. I don't understand. She liked having bare feet. Used to take her shoes off as soon as she could. And she always put them tidily away. I didn't give her a chance that night though. I found them in her cupboard. I don't suppose he put them there. I don't suppose he even knows which cupboard is hers.

I'm dozing a lot. I keep dreaming she's talking to me. Telling me things. She comes to me in my sleep, dressed like a spy. Like Mata Hari. The spy who loved me. We talk in my dreams. Talk like it's real.

We don't argue in my dreams.

She doesn't lie in my dreams.

Then I was in the bathroom, brushing my teeth, getting ready for her funeral. I was wearing black, not much makeup. I'd been crying. The room was very steamy so I opened the window and there she was. In the garden, picking strawberries. I ran down the stairs and outside. The grass was cold and wet on my bare feet. She turned and smiled at me. I was so happy.

"You're not dead. You're not dead!"

"No, but I am very sick, I've got to get this ready."

I looked down. I saw she wasn't picking strawberries but digging them up. Only she wasn't doing it right. She was digging too deep. She was digging her grave.

"No darling," I grabbed her arm "No. You don't have to be buried. You're not dead any more."

"But all the people are coming for my funeral. I can't let them down."

She wouldn't stop. She kept on digging. She was digging her grave and kept saying she had to hurry to finish in time for the funeral. She wouldn't listen to me. I was pulling on her arm, trying to pull her back into the house, but she wouldn't come. She wanted to keep digging.

I woke up. In a cold sweat. And then I realised I'd been dreaming. It was a dream. She wasn't digging her grave after all. And I felt so good, it meant she wasn't dead. I was crying with relief when I opened my eyes properly. And I saw her. And I knew she was right. Even in my dream she was right. She's always right.

I must have been sitting with her for a few days now. I know I should do something but I don't know what. My brain is very fuzzy and I can't work out what to do. I should call someone but I can't make up any sentences. And anyway, if I do call them, they'll take her away. They'll get what they always wanted. They'll take her away from me.

I try wishing. Knocking on wood. Even praying. But wishes are for the tooth fairy. And the prayers come out jumbled up.

"Hail Mary, Mother of God, pray for us sinners and lead us not into temptation, now and at the hour I lay me down to sleep, I pray the Lord my soul to keep, if I should die before I wake . . ."

But I don't, do I?

Her office must still think she's on holiday. I suppose she is.

It's Friday today. Again. Fridays are ghastly, and even now they bring their anxieties. For all I know she's probably arranged to meet someone for dinner. Her parents, or that man, John. Or someone else. Someone else from her fantasy life. Someone she "forgot" to tell me about, who gave her the excitement that I never could. I expect they'll call. Perhaps I should just unplug the phone completely. I can't stand the ringing. I want it to be quiet. Completely quiet. I want them all to leave me alone. To leave us alone.

I slept some more and then when I woke it was nearly dark again. I could see the street lamps through the crack in the curtains, their orange lights just beginning to warm up. She was still sitting there and I knew I had to go out. I couldn't sit there any more. I realised the time for waiting was over. I put on my coat and left.

Or tried to leave. But there you were on the doorstep.

And here we all are.
   Isn't it cold?

CHAPTER 28

Working it out

It was after ten before Maggie finally finished her story. Dolores had put her to bed and managed to persuade Saz not to call the police immediately.

"At least wait until we've heard what she has to say."

While Dolores was putting Maggie to bed, Saz dealt with September. She laid the dead weight out and covered her with a clean sheet. She murmured an apology to September for the way she half dragged her to the sofa and with memories of a Presbyterian childhood Sunday school was about to offer up a Lord's Prayer for her when she noticed a tiny menorah on the shelf,

"OK September, I know Maggie's Catholic, and I know this might be an ornament, but just in case I'll stick to the twenty third psalm – it belongs in both books."

She smoothed September's hair from her forehead and covered her with the sheet. It was only once she stood back and looked at the covered body that it occurred to her she should maybe have left it there for the police. She made sweet tea and took it in to the bedroom where Dolores was cradling Maggie and they listened to her explanations.

Eventually Maggie told herself out and fell asleep in Dolores' arms. They left her and went into the kitchen.

"Sorry about this Saz, I feel responsible for getting you involved in all this. God knows what Maggie's on about –

all this drug stuff and all these men – sounds crazy to me."

"Yeah, it sounded that way to me too, a couple of months ago. But it all makes perfect sense now."

"What?"

Saz made more tea and told Dolores her side of the story.

"And now I just feel like shit, because if I hadn't been playing detective when I met Maggie at that club, if I'd just have come out with it and asked her – maybe she wouldn't be a gibbering wreck now, and maybe if I'd been honest with you and Annie as soon as I got back from New York – well, maybe we wouldn't have to explain to the police why it took us three hours to call them."

"Call your friends then."

"What friends?"

"Your policewoman friends. At least they know some of the story already and they'll be able to convince their boys in blue of our innocence, if not Maggie's."

"Do you think she is innocent?"

"I think she hit her, but I don't think she killed her. Do you?"

"No. Or not intentionally anyway. There's missing money and there's the shoes. Maybe she woke up. And don't forget, I know Simon James. I know him and I'm scared of him. I'll call Helen and Judith."

The two women arrived looking tired with three other carloads of policemen, some plainclothes and several more in uniform, all of whom looked more than wide awake. Helen grabbed Saz as she came in the door.

"I bloody well hope you haven't got us all in shit here."

"Yeah, so do I Hells. But none of us are in as much trouble as Maggie. Or September for that matter."

Saz spent the rest of that night giving statements to the police. First at Maggie's flat, where they also got her to go over the whole process of exactly how she moved the body, at what time and why – a question Saz couldn't find a very good answer for, other than that she'd wanted to give the body some dignity. She then had to repeat the entire process again at the Stockwell police station. Dolores was questioned for the first couple of hours and then allowed to go. Maggie was rushed under police escort to hospital, the nights with no food, drink or heating and only the company of a dead lover having taken their toll.

Two policewomen escorted Saz back to her own flat, where they took all her notes about the case and then searched through the rest of her stuff for anything that might incriminate her. There was nothing. She asked if she could call John Clark to tell him the news herself, but was told to stay out of the matter completely, that under no circumstances was she to try to contact him and to report back to Stockwell police station at eleven that morning. It was already six thirty.

She ran herself a huge bath, almost unbearably hot and forced herself into the tub. She lay there as long as she could and when she came up from under the water she realised she was crying. She curled up in the water. Sobbing until all the tears were shaken out of her. She let the water out of the bath and lay there, feeling the weight of her own body come back to her. She dried herself and crawled into her bed, setting the alarm for ten. As she fell asleep she realised she'd called Maggie's girlfriend "September" all night and the police had referred to her as the deceased. She'd held her dead body and she still didn't know her name. She started crying again as she slipped into sleep.

Saz spent most of Saturday at the police station answering all the same questions she'd answered the night before.

She'd been told that as she wasn't under arrest she had no need of a lawyer. That she was just "helping with their inquiries" – she wondered how many times she'd heard that phrase on the radio and how often she'd assumed the person "helping" was the person who was guilty. She wondered how often the police made the same assumption. In the late afternoon they brought in an American who asked her questions about Simon James. He seemed to already know a lot about him, the questions were more in the way of confirmations than eliciting any information.

"So he had coke in his possession?"

"Did you ever see him give any to anyone else?"

"Did you meet any of the other women he used to courier drugs?"

It was only when he asked how long she'd worked for James that it occurred to Saz that the American thought she'd been running coke too.

"Listen, I only worked there as a hostess. And I only worked as a hostess so I could find out about the place. Find out about him. And if you're from the New York police, then it's a bloody shame you didn't bother to ask these questions earlier instead of assuming that a man with lots of respectable associates, not to mention lots of money, is also a respectable man, because if you had, September might have been alive today."

"Yes Ms Martin, it is a shame. It's also a shame you didn't contact us when you were in New York and then we might have kept him in the country. Now, if you don't mind, let's get on with this. One girl's already dead, there's plenty more where she came from. Hundreds of girls no doubt, all running small amounts of coke, all thinking they were the only ones and it wasn't really a big deal, just a few ounces here or there. But when you add it all up it is a big deal. So why don't we see if we can stop him now?"

By ten Saz and the American were both exhausted. He told her he thought he had enough and said she could go.

"But hey, don't leave town!"

She tried to find out about Maggie at the police station but couldn't get any definite answers, so she called Dolores.

"I don't know. From what the policewoman said at the hospital today I don't think they believe she did it. Maggie's problem is that she thinks she did. She hit her, ran out, came back, she was dead. It's an obvious assumption. At least it is if you're under a fair bit of strain in the first place."

"Well, have they charged her with anything?"

"Not yet. Apparently it's some kind of an offence not to notify the 'authorities' as soon as a living being turns into a dead one, but given Maggie's mental state I don't think they'll bother about it. What about your info? Have they got your Mr James yet?"

"No. Not that I think they'd tell me, I'm hardly their favourite person. But I think they're finally convinced that I'm not just his vindictive drug smuggling ex-girl-friend."

"Good work!"

"Yeah, well it's taken them most of the day to figure out I'm gay – they should have checked my bookshelf first. Anyway, I'm going home now – keep in touch?"

"Sure. We're partners in innocence remember?"

Saz caught the bus home. At her flat she ran up the stairs two at a time, slammed the door behind her and double-locked herself in. She flicked on all the lights, went through each room, looking in every cupboard, under the bed, behind every door. Twice. Only when she was certain she was alone in the flat did she close the curtains and switch off the lights.

She was about to get into bed when she heard the faint
slam of a car door. It wasn't unusual but she was still
feeling pretty jittery and decided to get out of bed anyway.
She pulled the curtain back just a little and looked down
into the car park. Leaning against a car and lighting a
cigarette was Simon James. He threw down his match and
looked up. Directly at Saz's window.

CHAPTER 29

Tidying up

The trial was long and tedious. Involving lots of transatlantic lawyering. Claire had to explain most of the intricate details, and none of it sounded anything like *LA Law*. Months after the day Saz had first seen September she finally said goodbye to Simon James.

She had called Helen as soon as she saw James in the car park and within five minutes the place was swarming with police and he'd been arrested.

James obviously had no idea that Saz was connected with September and Maggie or he'd never have made the mistake of going to her flat. He'd just decided to check up on her as he was in England. He'd had Carrie's flat broken into and the relevant info sent over to him. As Saz's address was in Carrie's diary for their lunch date the week before she went to New York and as her name was all through Carrie's first couple of weeks there, it was easy to put two and two together and come up with Saz's real name and London address. He'd dealt with one September, taken a couple of days off and decided to look up the other – probably to resume where they'd left off at their last meeting.

Proving he'd been in Maggie's flat the night of the murder was easy – there were fingerprints everywhere, including on the plastic bag that had contained John Clark's money. The autopsy proved September had died from an overdose of cocaine administered intravenously, which pretty much cleared Maggie. The police doctor said the bump on the head had knocked her out but not killed her, she'd probably woken up a couple of hours later – that would have been when she'd taken off her shoes and started to tidy up. Then someone else had come in and administered the "fatal dose". September was in the lounge, she would have tried to get up and fallen again. No wonder Maggie thought it was all her fault.

The hard part was proving that Simon James had anything to do with it. He openly admitted he had been in her flat, but maintained that was because he and September were occasional lovers and had been for years. Maggie had to sit there and listen to it all. Using the information Saz had stolen about the other "Septembers", the police were finally able to trace one of them and get a real witness to James' activities. When Judith interviewed her she admitted carrying coke for him three times before she couldn't stand it, or him, any longer and had gone to ground in Cumbria. Having been his sometime lover and having been threatened in the same way that September was when she tried to get out of the work, she was scared but finally persuaded to testify against James. She confirmed that his London business was used as a cover for smuggling, and told them about another business he had in Paris. For her and for Saz this meant days in court waiting to give just a couple of sentences in evidence, all the while the police were trying to stop James' lawyers taking him back to America.

In the end there wasn't enough evidence to convict him of murder, but he was extradited to the States to stand trial there on drug smuggling charges. Saz was treated to a New York trip at the expense of the United States Treasury in order to testify against him. There was a lot of fuss made about protecting Saz from any "connections" James may have had. A lot of fuss, but in the end very little was done. She was called to testify and then sent back to London. She had little choice. Having admitted to knowing much more than she should have in the first place and after "omitting" to tell the police what she knew and having worked illegally for James while she was in New York, she wasn't exactly in much of a position to make deals with the agents from the US government. Seven months later she heard he'd been jailed for eight years on drug offences. His businesses in both New York and Europe were closed down. Saz promised herself that she'd put extra locks on all her windows and took John Clark out to tell him the news.

"Yeah, I know Ms Martin, they told me when they gave me back my money."

"You got it back?"

"Not all of it, but quite a lot. Something to do with illegal proceeds from his business. I don't know. I think I was lucky to get anything out of it at all."

"How are you getting on?"

"Well, I've used most of the lump sum to set myself up in business – the same sort of thing I did for Telecom only freelance. Retraining work, conference kind of stuff."

"Your wife must be pleased?"

"Yeah, we had a bit of a hard time for a while, but we're working together on the business so it's been good for us. We like working with each other. She feels more secure about me, and I think I owe her that. I guess I must owe you too?"

"I don't think so, I don't think I made a very good job of any of this."

"Yes you did. If it hadn't been for you, they'd never have found him and your Maggie would have taken all the blame."

"Yeah, but I didn't exactly find September for you, did I?"

"You did."

"A little late."

"Better late than never."

"I don't suppose her family think so."

"No. I don't suppose Ms Simpson does either, and to tell the truth I can't say I'm happy about it, of course not, but the fact remains, that if it wasn't for you, she'd still be dead and Simon James McAuley would be running free. It may only be eight years, but it's something."

"I 'spose you're right."

"I know I am. Now here's the money I owe you, and I'm sorry it took so long."

"I don't think I can take it."

"Well, there it is. I think you earned it. I expect the drug squad do too. Goodbye Ms Martin."

John Clark left Saz in the café with the cheque on the table. It was the same café he'd met her in nine months earlier. She picked up the cheque. Two thousand five hundred pounds. She went straight out and put it in a high interest account where she wouldn't be able to touch it for three years.

"That'll please my mother. And hopefully by then I won't feel so sick about it."

As she went into the tube she passed a young woman with dyed blonde hair and a thin puppy tied on a string.

"Spare us twenty pence luv?"

Saz reached into her pocket and pulled out a fifty pound note.

"Here. Grow your hair out."

She gave her the money and went down the stairs into the tube.

CHAPTER 30

Afters

Dolores told Saz about the funeral.

"It was very quiet, cold really. Nothing like my grand-mother's funeral, with all of her old friends there. What was interesting though, was who turned up – we all went. All of her family of course, and even John Clark and his wife. We took Maggie with us. At least that's how we all arrived, once we'd separated into the men and women it looked a bit different though. Her dad, her brother-in-law, a bunch of her other male relatives and ex-boyfriends, together with John Clark, Keith and his son. And all of us women crowded together."

"How were the family with Maggie?"

"Well, how do you expect?"

"I don't know, I thought people always came round at times of great trial."

"Only in the movies, Saz. Anyway, I'm not sure if the parents even knew which one was Maggie. I introduced her to the sister though and she was quite civil – well, she had to be, the police had told her all the stuff that really happened, I think they gave the parents a watered down version of the little darling's antics in New York."

"You still don't like her much, huh?"

"How can I not like someone who's dead? No, I don't dislike her, but I think she gave Maggie a very hard time. I don't like this pretending. Any pretending. It can only end in tears. What she never understood was the good bits that come once the excitement's worn off. I don't think she ever really tried."

"Well, I can understand her desire for excitement. I certainly feel it."

"Yeah, sure. I don't deny that. I like excitement as much as the next girl. What I think is sad is that she never gave Maggie the chance to experience the 'passion of stability'."

"Sounds like you know all about it?"

"I'm trying to."

Saz kept in touch with Maggie and Dolores. Maggie was slowly getting better. After a month in hospital she moved back in with Annie and Dolores.

A year later Maggie took Saz to the cemetery.

"So, do you come here often?"

"At least once a fortnight. It's less to see her now, more to give me a chance to think – the house is still bloody busy. Especially now that Gillian's boyfriend has moved in. Keith still can't believe he managed to produce three heterosexual kids!"

"Is he nice?"

"Keith?"

"The boyfriend?"

"He's OK. For an American."

"Oh. Bad memories?"

"They're fading – and I thought I'd finished with therapy! This way. She's just over here."

Saz followed Maggie over to the new gravestone. She picked up a small stone from the ground.

"You have to put a stone on her. It's a Jewish thing. I'm not sure why, but she told me that's what you have to do."

She then took a small crumpled rose out of her pocket.

"I leave her a flower too. I don't think you're supposed to, but she likes roses. I don't suppose she'd mind. She liked bacon flavoured crisps as well."

She crossed herself and looked up at Saz.

"Nice headstone, isn't it?"

Saz took in the plain white stone and read what she could, one part was in Hebrew.

"What does it mean?"

"It's her name – Stav."

"Stav?"

"Yep, only most English people called her Steph."

"Yeah, I heard that at the trial, what does Stav mean?"

"It's Hebrew for autumn."

"Oh?"

"Yeah, her mother told me the story."

"You've been talking to her mother?"

"Once or twice, she's OK. We've met here a few times. Accidently, but I kind of like it. I think she does too. She's got some good stories."

"What's the story of her name then?"

"Well, they were living up north. Autumn comes sooner then, right?"

"Yeah."

"They'd been planning to go to Israel for a holiday, only her dad was working as a builder in those days and summer was a very busy time for them. They didn't have much money then and they'd put this holiday off for ages, so Sarah – her mother's called Sarah, of course – said that as soon as she saw the first yellow leaf on the tree in their garden then he'd have to take two weeks off. And she saw the leaf and they went away. He took the time off and she was conceived in Israel."

"And so they called her Stav because she wouldn't have happened but for the autumn leaves?"

"You're very quick."

"It's my job."

Maggie got up.

"Sorry, I've got to go now, sad movies always make me cry."

"Me too, thanks for bringing me."

"Sure. 'Bye."

Maggie was just walking away when a thought occurred to Saz.

"Hey Maggie, did Sarah say when she saw the yellow leaf?"

"Yeah. She said it meant she got a summer holiday in Israel after all. Well, late summer anyway. It was on the first of September."

Maggie carried on walking.

Saz picked up a stone from the graveside and placed it with all the others.

"Somehow I thought it might be."

**Also by Stella Duffy and published by
Serpent's Tail**

Wavewalker

"Very near the top of the new generation of crime writers"
The Times

"The clever money should be on Duffy when the crime-writing Oscars are dished out" *Telegraph*

"A feisty little page-turner guaranteed to keep you up all night" *Big Issue*

Saz Martin investigates the activities of Dr Maxwell North, an internationally acclaimed therapist, healer and guru.

Saz has been hired by a mystery employer – the Wavewalker – who walks at the edge of tides where the waves cover footprints and you can't tell if you're being followed or led. In an investigation which starts in seventies San Francisco and then comes crashing into her own nineties London life, the secrets of Dr North's healing "Process" and a surplus of suicides propel Saz into lethal territory and a highly compustible conclusion.

Beneath the Blonde

"Saz Martin is . . . an ebullient heroine of courage and wry wit . . . Duffy's third novel removes her from the category of 'promising' and confirms without doubt that she's very near the top of the new generation of modern crime writers" Marcel Berlins, *The Times*

"Stella Duffy's writing gets better with each book" Val McDermid, *Manchester Evening News*

"Always a pleasure to find a new Stella Duffy novel . . . a good read and highly recommended" *Diva*

Siobhan Forrester, lead singer of Beneath the Blonde, has everything a girl could want – stunning body, great voice, brilliant career, loving boyfriend. Now she has a stalker too. She can cope with the midnight flower deliveries and nasty phone calls, but things really turn sour when intimidation turns to murder.

Saz Martin, hired to seek out the stalker and protect Siobhan, embarks on a whirlwind investigation, travelling with the band from London to New Zealand, via the rest of the world. As jobs go, this one shouldn't be too hard, except Siobhan isn't telling the whole truth and Saz isn't sure she wants to keep the relationship strictly business.

Beneath the Blonde is the third Saz Martin thriller, following the highly acclaimed *Calendar Girl* and *Wavewalker*, and *Fresh Flesh*, her latest, confirming Stella Duffy's position at the forefront of the new wave of British crime fiction.

Fresh Flesh

Patrick Freeman, celebrity chef, with the legendary bad temper and the obligatory wild child wife ... Chris Marquand, adopted son of wealthy parents, a successful doctor, father-to-be ... Georgina Leyton, high-powered lawyer and a beautiful bitch who's as cool as they come ... Luke Godwin, owner of the hottest South London bar and a talent for scaring the life out of people with his mad rages. Four virtual strangers, unwittingly bound together by a dark secret from the past. And, after all these years, it's about to blow up in their faces.

Everything was going just fine for Saz Martin and her partner Molly. It is summer in London. They're having a baby and all looks right with the world. Saz has even stopped taking on any weird and wild cases. No more danger, just easy, steady work and tucked up in bed before midnight ... Yeah, right.

Fresh Flesh, Stella Duffy's latest Saz Martin thriller, is a high-paced ride across a contemporary London of glitzy offices, fancy restaurants, designer bars and damaged lives. It is also a frightening journey through the emotional ruins of the past, a tale of the sins of the fathers, and the mothers, and of the greatest theft of all.

Other Serpent's Tail titles of interest

Charlotte Carter

Rhode Island Red

Street Saxophonist and Grace Jones lookalike Nanette has a masters in French, an on-off boyfriend called Walter and a dead undercover cop in her apartment. But her life starts getting really complicated when she discovers $60,000 stuffed into her sax, the cop's ex-colleagues turn up and she's courted by that elegant older man who wants her to teach him everything she knows about Charlie Parker.

And who, or what is Rhode Island Red?

"Elegiac and musical . . . Nan is a wonderful character" Liza Cody

"Wholly delightful . . . the year's freshest crime debut" *GQ*

"Sharp, funny and beautifully underscored with jazzy prose riffs" *Good Housekeeping*

"Irresistible New York fable . . . sex and jokes and a love for jazz which blows hot, cool and true from beginning to end" *Literary Review*

"It's refreshing to find a heroine who has both a rock-solid moral centre and a sense of humour" *Sunday Times*

"Enough spirit to keep you turning till the final page" *The Voice*

Agnes Bushell

The Enumerator

Lamont Bliss came to San Francisco all right, but when they found him dead the flowers he wore weren't just in his hair – they were spilling out of every wound in his mutilated body.

What happened to Lamont should never have been any of Alex's business. She was just back from New Mexico and the main thing on her mind was choosing a new tattoo. Then Sean the enumerator came calling.

The enumerators were everywhere that year, sex surveyors tracking the spread of HIV in San Francisco. But when someone told the enumerator a little too much about their sex life – that's when the killing started.

Driven by passion and violence, soaked in fear and sex, *The Enumerator* offers the sharpest take on San Francisco since Dashiell Hammett's *Maltese Falcon*.

"Bushell's post-AIDS, alternative San Francisco – a rich stew of blood lust, hypocrisy and death, Star Trek reruns, queer outings, and a promise of love – proves as arresting as her tattooed heroine's foreground investigation into a gay murder imaginatively executed – corpse as floral display" *Guardian*

"A twisting, subtle thriller of San Francisco in the AIDS years. Bushell conveys wonderfully well the lurking anger and darkness beneath this most sophisticated of American cities" *GQ*

Diane Langford

Left for Dead

Montse Letkin works for the council. She's what you might call a snooper. Montse is getting so good at her job that her boss Gwendoline Rhodes – that's the one they used to call Red Gwen – has lined Montse up as her personal security consultant. Montse wasn't so good at that though – Gwendoline fell out of a high window. And it would suit a lot of people if Montse took the rap.

In Montse Letkin, Diane Langford has created a heroine of our times, a bruised and cynical young woman learning the hard way that the personal really is political.

Left for Dead is a taut thriller set in London about ten minutes into the future. In a city where privatisation is the watchword and politics a dirty word. In a city where the weak and the homeless had best fend for themselves. In a city of secrets and lies, the legacies of the past collide in a unsettling, visionary slice of millennial noir.

George P. Pelecanos

A Firing Offense

As the advertising director of Nutty Nathan's – "The Miser Who Saves You Money!" – Nick Stefanos knows all the tricks of the electronics business. Blow-out sales and shady deals were his life.

When one of the stockboys disappears, it's not news: just another metalhead who went off chasing some dream of big money and easy living.

But the kid reminded Nick of himself twelve years ago: an angry punk hooked on speed metal and the fast life. So when the boy's grandfather begs Nick to try to find the kid, Nick says he'll try.

A Firing Offense, Nick Stefanos' debut, shows why George P. Pelecanos is a cult figure in U.S. crime writing. As Barry Gifford puts it, "To miss out on Pelecanos would be criminal."

"A contemporary classic . . . Pelecanos is a fresh, new, utterly hardboiled voice. *A Firing Offense* is full of virtuoso scenes of imaginative sex and substance abuse, suspenseful action, and brooding meditation on a newly lost generation" *The Washington Post*

"Pelecanos puts together a slam-bang climax that contains all the requisite elements – action, tragedy, victory, and random death. It's a terrific start for a quality series" *Mostly Murder*

George P. Pelecanos

Nick's Trip

"The coolest writer in America" *GQ*

"The kind of book you are always hoping to find but rarely do" James Sallis

"Here is your first turn-of-the-century crime writer" Charlie Gillett

"An even more promising follow-up to Pelecanos' highly recommended first novel, *A Firing Offense . . .*" *New Mystery*

"Snaps with authentic street talk and with a switch-hitting plot . . . has something important to say about trust and treachery" *Washington Post*

Nick Stefanos, having earned his P.I. license, quickly discovers that snapping photos of unfaithful husbands does not make for a fulfilling job. Tending bar one night at the Spot, Nick is visited by his high-school friend, Billy Goodrich. Billy's wife is gone. Nick agrees to find her. And with that first step, he sets out on a one-way trip through a sewer of theft, intrigue and love.

George P. Pelecanos' reputation goes from strength to strength.

George P. Pelecanos

Down by the River Where the Dead Men Go

After a night of drinking, Nick Stefanos passes out in a public park. Some time before dawn he wakes up when he hears a car door slam, and then a voice "You already been a punk. Least you can do is go out a man." Then a dull popping sound and a quiet splash.

And that's how Stefanos gets drawn into the murder of Calvin Jeter. The investigation takes him through the roughest part of the nation's capital and the blackest parts of the human soul.

Down by the River Where the Dead Men Go is the third title in the Nick Stefanos series – which establishes George Pelecanos as the rightful heir to the noir tradition of James Cain, David Goodis and Jim Thompson.

"The customers at the Spot in Southeast D.C. like to hear Barry White and Isaac Hayes on the bar's cassette player, but when they've all gone home, bartender Nick puts on P.J. Harvey. In his wallet is a state license which says he's Nicholas J. Stefanos, Private Investigator . . . George Pelecanos has broken with tradition in so many ways, it feels as if he has launched a category of his own. Partly, it's his convincing evocation of an unfamiliar setting but mainly it's the feeling that we are definitely in the present – here is your first turn-of-the-century crime writer."
Charlie Gillett